Love Conquer

BATTLEFIELD OF LOVE BOOK #3

CARY HART

Love Conquer (Battlefield of Love Series, #3)
Copyright © 2018 by Cary Hart.
Second Edition: December 2018

Cover designed by Sarah Paige of Opium House Creatives
Editing provided by Dani Hall of DMH Editing Services
Book formatting provided by Juliana Cabrera of Jersey Girl Design

All rights reserved. Printed in the United States of America. No part of this book may be used or reproduced in any manner whatsoever without written permission except in the case of brief quotations embodied in critical articles or reviews.

This book is a work of fiction. Names, characters, businesses, organizations, places, events and incidents either are the product of the author's imagination or are used fictitiously. Any resemblance to actual persons, living or dead, events, or locales is entirely coincidental.

Books by Cary Hart

BATTLEFIELD OF LOVE SERIES
Love War
Love Divide
Love Conquer

SPOTLIGHT COLLECTION
Play Me
Protect Me
Make Me (Coming Soon)
Own Me (2019)

THE FOREVER SERIES
(Coming January 2019)
Building Forever
Saving Forever
Broken Forever
Finding Forever

Brittany—
This book is just as much yours as it is mine.
Thank you for taking this journey with me and
for "calming me the f*ck down!"
#coffeesaveslives

Playlist

Praying by Kesha
Go Your Own Way by Lissie
The Other Side by Ruelle
War of Hearts by Ruelle
Don't Wanna Love You by Colbie Caillat
Weapons by Mark Diamond
Kindly Calm Me Down by Meghan Trainor
Monsters by Ruelle
Fall Harder by Fractures
Dusk Till Dawn by Zayn & Sia
I'll Survive You by BC Jean
Shine by LOLO
Bruises by Lewis Capaldi
Slow Motion by Matt Wertz
I Would Die 4 U by Noah Guthrie

NINA

When do the words "I'm sorry" mean nothing? His words hurting more than his touch? What happens when leaving is harder than staying?

Fear.

The lines between right and wrong have become so blurred... but accepting who you've become is not an option.

Shame.

Escape is the only way to fight back.

Hope.

"Miss?" A scratchy voice brings me out of my fog. "You gettin' in or not?" the driver from the taxi service demands.

"Huh? Oh, I-I umm...I don't know." My eyes scan the vehicle as realization sets in. *This is it.* I don't have another choice. Uber? Out of the question. He could track me. The bus services? I would have to show my ID. This is my only way out.

"I don't have all night." He leans forward, eyeing me through the rolled-down window of the taxi that has seen better days. Rusted and worn.

"I'll pay you. Just give me a minute, please..." I cut off the driver. "If you leave, I'm not sure if..." My voice trembles as I search for the words I *need* to say, but can't get out. Shaking it off, I take a deep breath, exhaling a plea, "Please, don't leave me here."

Settling back in his seat, he slides the seatbelt over his chest, and I hear the sound of metal popping into place, securing my fate.

He's going to leave.

One hand on the wheel, the other reaching to power up the window. Panic starts to set in. This was my last chance. *If* I stay... *Fight, Nina. Fight!*

"Hey!" I shout taking a couple of steps forward, slapping my hand over the window.

"You break it, you pay for it. Got it?" He seems more irritated than pissed.

"I'm sorry. I just need to..." I lean in, silently begging for a minute.

"Oh shit!" His voice raises an octave, something I've heard one too many times. "Girl, what happened to you?" The driver is now concerned.

Never hesitating, excuse mode always on, I pull the hood back over my head. It must have fallen down while I was trying to stop him. "Nothing. Just a run-in with a wall." I cover the bruise that is more purple than black and laugh. "Clumsy as hell." I turn, ashamed at the lies that are so easily spoken.

"If you say so." His hands grip the steering wheel a little tighter and he forces a smile across his face. "Alright kid, ten minutes."

"Thanks." I lower my head and back away.

I look over my shoulder, the house I tried to make a home, out of sight. Nothing but streetlights and dark skies.

Love Conquer

I tried to be the person he wanted but something changed, and for once I realize it wasn't me. What happened, it's not my fault.

So, why does it hurt?

Tilting my head back, I close my eyes, taking in the crisp air of the night, and ask for the strength to say goodbye to the life I thought I wanted. The one that destroyed me, killed my soul.

I don't want to forget. Forgetting means forgiving, and that means staying.

I can't.

I won't.

This is my new reality. I have no choice but to leave.

Survival.

Throwing my bags over my shoulder, I head toward the taxi. The driver is already out and popping the trunk.

"I just have these two." I throw one bag at a time in the backseat. "It's all I got." Those words speak more truth than I'm willing to admit.

"Well, I guess we are ready to go." He slams the trunk and hops back in.

"I guess so," I whisper and slide into the car next to my bags.

Adjusting the mirror, he glances at me; a look of understanding is there, but brief. Reaching down, he zeros out the meter. "This ride is on me."

"I can't..."

"Yes, you can and you will. No questions asked." He nods. "You got it?"

I want to tell him how thankful I am, but I can't. So, I just nod.

"It's a three-hour drive. I can be there a little under." He reaches over to the passenger's seat and rummages around in a bag. "Here it is." He tosses a flannel throw blanket back to me. "Get some rest. You look like hell." He puts the car into gear and we head to the one place I know I will be safe.

"No! Please stop." I freeze, afraid to run. The last time I tried to escape, he accidently pushed me too hard and I fell down a small flight of stairs, breaking my foot. "Brandon, I-I can explain."

"How do you think you can explain two thousand dollars missing from our savings account?" He holds up the bank statement, too close for me to read. His hands tremble from the anger I know he holds inside.

"I signed up for some classes," I whisper.

"Classes? Classes! Why in the fuck do you think you need to take classes? For what?" He throws the papers in my face. "You gonna leave me? Is that what you're doing?" He paces the floor. "That's it, isn't it?"

"Brandon, no! I promise. You know how I have always wanted to do interior des—" I start to say as I move closer to him, hoping if I can just get him to see me, he will come back.

Swinging around, he shouts, "Interior design? Interior fucking design? You spent the money on learning to paint?" His hands are in his hair, yanking, before he turns from me and knocks the lamp off the end table. His chest is rising and falling quickly. The beast is in there, ready to come out.

"Brandon...please..." I put my hand on his shoulder to show him I'm here to stay.

"What?" He turns, placing his hand on top of mine before he

Love Conquer

grabs my wrist. Squeezing in between the vice grip of his thumb and fingers, he brings it back to my side. "That money was to cover the bill for your broken foot." *He steps forward, right on to my bare foot, his steel-toe boot digging deep.*

"I have till next week to drop out, I'll get it back."

"Is that how you think it works? Really? How stupid are you? You can't get a refund." *His eyes are void of emotion, a wicked smirk plastered on his face.* "Get on your knees," *he orders.*

"Wh-what?"

"You're going to pay me back." *He nods to the floor.*

"Brandon..."

"Now!"

"Kid, wake up! Hey, you need to wake up." I feel a hand on my arm and jerk away in fear. "Aw hell, kid."

"I'm sorry. I-I...I was having a bad dream." I sit up straight, suddenly realizing we are on the side of the road. "Ummm..."

"Don't worry, you're safe. I'm sorry I touched your arm like that, I just couldn't get you awake. I was a little freaked." He turns back around, only looking at me through the rearview mirror. "I figured whatever happened, you would want a minute to gather yourself before we get to where you are going.

"Umm, yeah, thanks." I run my hands over my face. Clearing my thoughts, but mostly to hide from the embarrassment.

"We are just around the block. You ready?"

"Sure." *Am I?*

"Hey kid..." He throws his arm over the back of the seat and turns. "Are you sure you, this is where you want to go?" His eyes soften. "Cause I can take you somewhere...safe."

"Nina."

"You got it. I just need her house number." He turns back

13

around, ready to enter the numbers into his GPS.

"No, my name, it's Nina." I hold out my hand, "and..."

"Benny. My name is Benny and you..." He faces me and takes my hand, giving it a soft squeeze. "Need to talk to someone. Just promise you will talk to someone. I have daughters...if they looked—"

"I will," I cut him off. I can't deal with this. Not now. I'm here and that is all I can do.

"Okay." He breaks the contact and swings his door open and gets out. I watch him open the back door and grab my bags.

"I got those." I jump out and run around to his side of the car, grabbing the bags from his hands. "You have already done so much."

"I'm not leaving. Not until I see you make it in okay." He crosses his arms and leans back on the rusted, beat-up cab.

"I'm fine..."

"It's 4 a.m. Not fine." He smiles, waiting for my reaction.

"Ohhhh, well, maybe just until they answer the door." My smile is weak. "Benny, thank you."

"Don't even mention it." He winks.

Turning toward the house, I adjust the bags on my shoulders and take a small step, then another, and another. Each one is easier than the last. I drop the bags and take off running toward the door. The desperation overcomes me. The shadows are too close. I jiggle the handle, pounding on the door, needing to be freed.

"Who in the hell..." I hear her before I can see her. The door swings open. "Nina?"

Falling into her arms, I know everything will be okay. This is where I belong.

Love Conquer

Safe.

Chapter 1

NINA

Feeling the warmth of the sun kissing my face, I pull the covers up to hide for just a few more minutes. Sulking in bed is my new favorite pastime. Hiding behind the room-darkening shades...

"Hey!" I throw the covers off and quickly sit up. I see my sister, Niki, curled up on the chaise lounge in the corner. Knees to her chin, her sweater pulled over, and of course a freshly brewed cup of coffee snuggled between her hands.

Shrugging her shoulders, she brings her favorite mug to her lips and downs it. Typical Niki. She doesn't care how hot, what kind or how it's prepared. Sipping coffee is for "weak-ass bitches" — her words, not mine.

"You know, you are way more than a *coffee whore* right now." I point at her. "How about you close the curtains on your way out?" I fall back into the pile of pillows, ready to wait her out. I keep my eyes focused on the ceiling, avoiding her stare. If I stay just like this, she will eventually have to leave to get ready for work.

Okay bad plan. The sun, it's too bright and my skin feels like it's on fire. How in the hell do dogs stand lying in this crap?

Love Conquer

Turning my head to the side, I blink a few times and rub the warm spot on my face.

9:36 AM

She's late. I turn back toward her and our eyes meet.

Not saying a word, she untangles her legs from her sweater and stands, just looking at me. I've seen this expression too many times in the past month. Placing the mug on the dresser, she takes the few steps she needs to be at my side. "Nina..."

Here it comes. The lecture she gives me every morning. *"Nina, you need to either get up and talk about what happened or do something about it."*

Feeling the bed dip, I roll over to defuse the bomb for one more day, "Niki, please. Just a little more time. I promise, I'm dealing the only way I...Niki?"

This isn't the bomb. This is something more. Something I haven't seen since our parents' funeral. Niki crying. Silent tears streaming down her face. "I don't know how to help you. Every day I try, and each day you say you are dealing the only way you know how, but you aren't. I'm losing you, Nina." Her soft hands cradle my face. "You are the only family I have left. You can't leave me. You got it? I need you to snap out of this. I need *you* to talk to *me...please.*"

My sister, the strongest woman I have ever known, sassy and fierce, a force to be reckoned with, is breaking down and it's my fault. Niki Sanders is as strong and confidant as they come, but right now, she's desperate. Desperate for me to let her in, but even though I'm seeing her like this, I'm not sure if I can.

"Did you call off work because you were worried about me?" Of course, she is worried. My life for the past three years has been a total lie. Even the good times we had, in the beginning, were fake. The man I thought I knew never existed. I know that now.

"It's Tuesday. I only work when Gavin is short at the club, but that's not the point. You need to get up." She lifts her cashmere-covered arm to her face, wiping the tears away. Her mask is back on, the fight in her is back.

Wait? Did she say Tuesday?

"The club? What about school?"

"Oh, hell no!" She jumps up and flings the covers off of me. "I knew you were out of it, but this...I'm not letting you travel this path any longer. Up!"

"Hey! Give them back!" I desperately try to reach for something to cover myself up.

"Look at you, Nina." She looks around the room then stalks over to the mirror hanging by the door. She pulls it and the nail it hung from off the wall and returns to my side. "Look at you! Do you see who you have become?"

Looking at her, but avoiding my reflection, I reply, "I don't need to see myself, I know."

"Dammit! Look at yourself." She slaps her hand down on the mirror. Her ring hits against it, causing the glass to crack. "You don't eat, you haven't been outside. You're weak and frail."

"Niki, please."

"Now!"

A knock on the door interrupts her, but Niki's eyes are locked in on mine. Daring me to look.

"Everything okay in here?" Gavin Shaw, Niki's fiancé, questions.

I know if I so much as look away, I'm liable to end up on the floor in an arm bar, a move from one of the self-defense classes she has taken.

"We're fine," we yell in unison.

"Niki, remember, she's your sister." Gavin glances at me, giving me a small smile, before he turns to leave.

"Yes. She. Is." She tilts her head, her long, chestnut locks falling to the side.

If I didn't know her so well I would fight this battle, but with Niki, you never win.

"Fine." I whisper, bringing my eyes to the mirror.

This can't be. I reach my hand out, running it over the lines of my body. *Who have I become?*

Looking down, I take the same hand and touch my body. My once athletic frame is now a shell of what it once was. Since meeting Brandon, I was on a mission to lose weight, wanting to satisfy him. From physical to career to personal, appearance was everything to him. This should have been a red flag, but when you love someone, you look beyond, right? Weak and pale, bones bulging, I don't recognize the girl who sits here. But I'm the girl in the mirror. I'm her.

"Nina, it's Tuesday." She sets down the mirror. "It's June, school is out for the summer."

"What?" I push myself up. "June?"

"You've been here for three weeks. Now, get your ass up." She walks over to the dresser and starts grabbing some clothes, throwing them on the bed. "I gave you the time you needed. Today, your time is up."

"Okay. You're right." I throw my legs over the side of the bed and stand.

"Of course, I am." She stops to smile at me, hands on her hips. "Next time don't doubt me. Now go shower."

"Okay."

A shower will do me some good. Sliding on my slippers I pad over to the chair where I left my towel yesterday. "Where's my towel?"

"You mean the one from Saturday? It's in the wash and if you are wondering what that smell is...it's you!"

Walking past her, I stick my tongue out. I hate it when she is right. Mentally checking off the days, as I head to the bathroom, I realize it has been three days since I took one.

"New towel and washcloth are on the sink and your makeup is on the counter. Be ready in an hour," she shouts after me.

Peeking out, I ask, "An hour?"

"We are going for coffee. Aubrey had to cancel and, well, you know how I get if I don't get my fill. So, no excuses." She looks down at her watch. "Make that fifty-five minutes. You're moving too slow."

Being a tad overdramatic, for the ultimate sister experience, I roll my eyes and let out a whoosh of a sigh. All in her line of vision. After all, that's what little sisters are for.

After shutting the door, I reach my hand into the shower and turn on the water. As the steam begins to fill the room, I begin to undress, catching my reflection. *How did I not notice?* Three weeks of walking around numb to my surroundings. Somewhere down the road, I lost who I was.

Leaving was one of the hardest decisions I've ever made. How do you say goodbye to someone you once loved, without it affecting you? It was supposed to set me free, not cage me in my own fears. If I continue like this, living a life in pain, I let him win and I refuse to believe my struggles were in vain.

The mirror begins to fog and my reflection vanishes. "Just

like I did." My voice barely audible. If I wouldn't have spoken the words, I wouldn't have known I said them. I didn't get to say goodbye, I escaped from Brandon, but not the fears that followed me.

Niki is right. I need to talk to somebody. The past three years, I have been told who I can and can't talk to. Today, I'm giving myself a choice. I may not be ready to talk today, but that is *my* choice, but what I am ready for.

Acceptance.

I can't undo my past, but I can change my future.

Chapter 2

NINA

I CAN'T WAIT FOR YOU to try this place. The coffee here at Java Talk is orgasmic. Like seriously, Nina. Once you take a drink, you mouth will literally form an 'O'," Niki fires off another random thought.

All the way here she has talked about everything from school to the color of that car. Was it a midnight blue or navy blue? I still don't know.

"I think you're the only one who would orgasm over coffee."

"You think? Cause I'm pretty sure this coffee would put the vibrator out of business." Niki flashes me her perfect smile.

"I worry about you." I reach for the door, holding it open, announcing her presence. "All hail the Queen of Coffee."

"Aren't you forgetting something?" she chuckles.

"You totally just ruined the moment." I bring my fist up and cough. "Greedy bitch." I cough again.

"I heard that, but if I'm royalty you should bow." She says as people walk around our little show.

"Your highness." I hold out my arms and do a little curtsey, sticking my butt out a little more than necessary to keep the door open.

Love Conquer

"Much better." She walks through the door pointing to the barista working the counter. "Jen, coffee me!"

"You got it! The usual?" she hollers back.

"Give me two screaming O's." Niki winks everyone turns to look at her. She scans the crowd in disbelief. "Oh come on? Am I the only one who loves coffee *that* much?" she dares them to reply. "Oh well, you don't know what you're missing. This shit is the bomb dot com, yo!"

All this is too much. Everyone is staring. I back out of the doorway, letting the door fall shut, remaining outside so I can breathe.

In. Out. In. Out.

I watch through the glass, and things seem to be back to normal. The door opens and closes as customers leave with their to-go orders.

"Miss, you coming or going?" The deep timbre of a man's voice causes me to jump. Looking up, I see part of his reflection in the glass, taller than me by half a person. Okay maybe I'm exaggerating, but he's way over six foot.

"Uhhh..."

"Well, I'm grabbing some orders to go, but first, I really need to use the facilities." He responds to my inability to talk and takes a step forward, reaching over me to open the door. "So, if you could..."

"Oh, yeah of course. I-I...I'm going in, thanks." I keep my head down and walk in and straight over to where Niki is sitting.

"It's about time. What were you doing over there?" Niki looks down at her phone.

"Switch me sides." I'm bouncing from foot to foot, needing

23

to be out of sight. What happened out there was embarrassing. I couldn't even speak.

"Sure." She gets up and plops down on the other side of the table and I fall into her previous seat.

"Thanks. I was zoning out outside and, well, this guy walked up..." I reach for one of the cups of coffee.

"Hey!" She smacks my hand. "Get your own. These are mine." She reaches out and pulls both cups closer to her.

Rubbing my hand, I give her my best *screw you* look.

"I'm serious. I've already paid. Just go up to the counter and Jen will hook you up with a coffee and danish. They are to die for." She takes a huge gulp, making an "O" face. Probably for my benefit. "That reminds me...a bakery down the road has these hazelnut glazed croissants that are panty-melting delicious."

"Seriously, do you have to make sexual comparisons?"

"I totally don't." She stops herself. "Okay, so maybe I do. But if you just tried them you would get what I was saying." She shoos me off. "You better hurry, they only had a couple left."

"Fine." I edge out of my seat, scanning the counter for Mr. Tall Guy.

Coast is clear.

"Only two!" Niki calls out.

Stopping, I look over my shoulder and mouth. "Okay."

"Hurry," she mouths back, her eyes wide.

I make my way to the counter.

"You must be Nina. Hey girl." The barista beams behind the counter.

"Yep. And you must be Jen." I have no choice but to mirror her smile.

"That's me." She reaches for a cup and a Sharpie, writing my

Love Conquer

name down. "What can I get you?

"I'll just take what my sister had plus a cream-cheese danish."

"Good choice." She begins to fiddle with the machine. "So how long are you here for?"

Deciding Jen isn't so bad, I lean my hip on the counter, welcoming the conversation. "I'm here to stay."

"Oh, that's wonderful." She reaches for the milk. "Nonfat?"

"Sure."

Filling the small metal pitcher with the skim milk, she holds it under the steamer, pressing the button. "Dang it." Her face begins to flush as she presses the button repeatedly and mutters curses.

"Need some help?" I lean over the counter just as the machine kicks on and a big burst of steam comes out, spraying the milk all over the front of her.

"Ugh! I swear, why does this stuff always happen to me?" She slams the pitcher down and removes her apron. "I must have kicked a puppy in my younger years because stuff like this only happens to assholes who are mean to puppies. Right?" Jen reaches into a drawer behind her and pulls a new apron on over her head and grabs a new cup.

I can't help it. A laugh rolls out. "Kick a puppy?"

"Well, yeah." She looks up as she pours the milk for a second time. "What's worse than that?"

"You got me there." I watch her go for the machine for a second time. "Wait! You need to clean that."

"I got a new pitcher." She holds it up. "See? Clean."

"No, the duct in the spout needs cleaned." I'm practically sitting on the counter now, but still can't reach. "Can I come around?"

"Sure." She flips the counter up. "By all means, help yourself."

"See, the trick to having a successful day is to not have the milk touch the opening of the spout. Let the pressure push the steam throughout the pitcher, warming the milk." I unscrew the parts and examine each one.

"You look like you know what you're doing." Jen stands behind me, looking over my shoulder.

"I used to work at a Starbucks when I was in nursing school."

"You're a nurse? Niki didn't mention that."

"I dropped out."

"That sucks. Why?" She asks a simple question, but in all reality, I have no clue what I should say. *"My boyfriend thought it would save us money?" "He was a controlling asshole who didn't want me to make a living for myself, afraid I may leave?"* Yeah, those don't go over well so I stick with the norm.

"It wasn't for me." I find the clogged filter. "See, dried milk is clogging the spout." I bang it against the counter to rid it of the crud and hand it over. "Wash this out, screw it back on and you will be good to go."

"Huh. Well looky there, learn something new every day." She reaches over to turn on the sink to let it fill. "You know, we are looking for help." She points to a handcrafted sign made out of coffee beans. "You would be the perfect fit, plus you get to work with lil' ol' me." She bats her eyelashes as she sticks her hands in the water. "Crap, I forgot the hot water is broke. The plumber won't be in till tonight." She looks around. "I'm just going to run to the back to clean this out and grab more whip. You stay there and think about the job offer."

Flipping up the counter, I head back to the other side to

Love Conquer

wait. "I'll be here."

Taking a step back, I rest against the half wall, taking in my surroundings. There is a high-schooler sitting alone, staring out the window. I can't help but wonder why. Did she have a fight with her parents? Is she waiting for her boyfriend? Maybe she is applying for a job and is waiting on the manager?

Then a couple tables down there are two girls in their early twenties, probably my age, and a guy. The blonde who is sitting next to the guy is being really affectionate. Holding his hand with one hand while reaching over with the other to rub his arm. The brunette sitting across the table looks in every direction but at them, until the blonde reaches to answer her phone and I swear the brunette mouths, "*Tell her.*"

I guess I never really paid attention before, but as I stand here observing these customers, it really makes me wonder, did anybody know? Could they see what I was going through? Were they watching me, like I'm watching these people?

My eyes land on Niki and she holds up her hands. I signal it will only be a few more minutes when something familiar grabs my attention.

In the booth behind Niki sits a woman, facing away from the window, and a guy, probably her husband, sits beside her. Her hands pull at the arms of her long-sleeved shirt, a shirt that is too warm for early summer. Probably hiding bruises from last night. Out of the corner of her eye, she notices me.

As she turns we make eye contact, a silent conversation, her pleading for me to help. It's an SOS I have signaled so many times, but always left unsaved. Her husband notices, and looks between us. He whispers something in her ear. I shake my head for her not to go and nod toward the bathroom. Maybe

I couldn't be saved, but I'll be damned if she walks out of here with him. He stands, hand on her elbow, pulling her with him. The sound of a palm connecting to the counter causes me to jump.

"Jen, I got one hell of an order for you."

It's him.

I freeze, startled like a deer in headlights, paralyzed.

"You okay?" Mr. Tall Guy reaches for my arm.

"Don't touch me." I jerk away, not seeing Jen holding out my coffee. "Shit!" The coffee drops to the floor and splatters all over my legs.

"I didn't mean to..." he utters.

"Nina! You okay?" Niki is by myside. "Kyle, what did you do to her?" Great. Niki knows Mr. Tall Guy.

"Absoluting nothing, Niki, so, you can leave my balls intact. Got it?" He laughs, smiling over at me, but I'm not in the mood to return it.

"I'm just going to the bathroom to clean up." I turn and notice the empty booth.

They're gone. I run to the bathroom and check under all the stalls hoping she is hiding out, waiting for me. With each empty stall, my hope fades. *She's gone.*

Taking a handful of towels, I clean up my legs and head back out to see Jen, who is mopping up the floor, while Niki puts out *Wet Floor* signs. I may not have been able to save her today, but maybe, just maybe, she will be back tomorrow.

"The job offer still stand?" I blurt out, shocking both Jen and Niki.

"Sure does." Jen stops, placing the mop back in the bucket.

"Good, I need an application."

Love Conquer

"No need. Can you start tomorrow?" She grabs a business card and writes down some information.

"Yep."

"Good. My uncle owns Java Talk. So, if I say you're hired, you're hired." She hands over the card. "Here is my number and your hours for the week."

I look down at the card. "Dang, that's early."

"In early, leave early. Plus, you get free coffee." She winks.

"Free coffee? Jen, you holding out on me?" Niki interrupts, and we all laugh.

Waving the card in the air, I say, "I'm glad I met you. See you tomorrow."

"Me too. Till tomorrow."

"You ready to go?" Niki asks. "Gavin wants us to come to Spotlight for lunch."

"Show me the way."

Chapter 3

KYLE

"Damn, man. Forget the coffee, it's almost time for lunch," Drew blurts out over the Bluetooth.

I mentally flip off my best friend and boss, owner of WilliamSon Construction. I'm more than just the lead foreman. Hell, he's asked me time and time again if I want to be partners, but this job, it's just that: a job that keeps me busy during the day. My personal projects, well, they get worked on during the night.

"Blame your wife," I fire back as I drive down the rock road of our new remodel. "Her, and Niki's sister."

"What's Aubrey have to do with this?" I know curiosity is getting the best of him. "Oh, and stay away from Niki's sister. Niki texted Aubrey to have her text me to remind you to stay away. What's up with that?"

"Aubrey's fault for that new protein drink. Let's just say my wait time at Java Talk was a little longer than expected." I know he knows what I'm talking about. Ever since she found out she was pregnant with their son, she has been on this healthy kick making Drew drink these healthy shakes and since I gave him hell, he had her send a case to my house too. Not cool, bro.

Love Conquer

"Say no more." He cracks up on the other end of the line. "But what about Niki's sister?"

"I ran into her at Java Talk." I recall the before and after. "Something happened and she freaked out. Niki came over and thought it was me, but before I could say too much, she ran to the bathroom and didn't come back out. But don't worry. Niki informed me that was her sister and to keep my hands off."

"Good. Then consider this talk my warning." His laughter fades. "I'm serious, Lewis."

"I'm pulling in. Send those twerps down to get their girly lattes." I press end, ignoring his "warning." Truth be told, something about that girl intrigues me.

Putting my truck into park, I open the door and hop down, looking around for Lee and the rest of the guys to show up, but none of them come. *Thanks, Drew.* I may have gotten stuck getting their coffee for the week because of one little hazing prank, but I'll be damned if I hand deliver each and every one.

Heading to the back of the truck, I open up the steel toolbox and pull out my belt, along with my safety equipment.

Grabbing a box of nails, I throw on my hardhat and head to find Drew to get the rundown.

"Hey, Lewis, it's about time you got here." He looks around. "Where's the coffee?"

"Out in the truck. I only have so many hands, man. They can get it—"

Before I can finish, Drew brings his fingers to his lips, letting out a whistle, signaling for the crew to take a break.

"Hey, boss." Lee is the first to enter. "Where's the—"

"Out in the truck," I cut him off.

Lee is an eager employee. Always the first one here and

31

ready to work, volunteering on the weekends to prep the site. Drew really lucked out in finding him, but sometimes I like to give him a hard time and it doesn't sit well with Drew. So, that is how I ended up buying six-dollar coffees for Lee and his crew for a whole week.

"Got it." He walks past me, hardhat off.

"Hey, Lee? Where's your hat?" I call after him.

"On the second level," he shouts back.

"Hat stays on till you get in your truck. You got it? I have one in the back."

"Got it, boss." He opens the truck, grabs the hat, puts it on and comes back with the coffee. The others come running out to grab theirs.

"Man..." Drew walks up behind me and places his hand on my shoulder. "Take it easy. The crew know all about safety. They have watched the videos. They're good." He gives me a little pat. "I promise."

Exhaling a breath I didn't know I was holding, I begin to apologize, but the buzzing of my phone interrupts my train of thought.

The phone blinks: *Mom Calling*

"Hey Mom," I sigh into the phone.

"That's no way to greet your momma." She chuckles. "Hard day at work?"

"Actually, it just started."

"Is everything okay?" She sounds concerned.

"Yeah, it is." I walk down the steps and take a seat on one. "Listen, Mom, I know why you're calling and I'll be there."

"Oh good. I was so afraid you wouldn't show. Jimmy misses having you come around," she says of my stepdad, who has been nothing but a great father to me and my stepbrother Jack.

My father, William "Woody" Lewis, died after an accident at work. He was helping unload some wood at his lumber yard but the employee using the forklift didn't see him and smacked him in the head with a lift full of two by fours. He was knocked unconscious, and died later at the hospital from an epidural hematoma and swelling in his brain. My mom was the one who had to make the decision to pull the plug. They could have kept him on machines, but he was basically braindead. Any hope of having a life, gone. They said if he would have been wearing his hardhat, he would have survived.

My mom, Brenda, ended up in grief counseling a year later, where she met Jimmy Bennett, whose wife died of stage 4 breast cancer around the same time my dad died.

"I know Mom. I'll be there. Listen, I have to go. Drew needs help measuring something."

"Okay, son. Make sure everyone is wearing a hardhat."

Standing up, I look around and see the crew is following orders, even Lee.

"Always. Love you," I reassure her.

"You too."

I press end and stuff the phone in my back pocket.

"I'm curious, what do you need to help me measure?" Drew comes out of nowhere.

"Nothing. Just needed to get off the phone. My mom was hounding me about the party again." I stride past him, to the white board. "Where we at?"

"Didn't sound like she was hounding you."

"OK, so I didn't really give her the chance. I gave her what she wanted before she even asked."

"I see." Drew pulls out his phone and smiles. "Aubrey is showing the girls how to make tacos tonight if you want to come over for dinner."

"Sounds like a family night." I want more than anything to say yes, to experience what Drew gets every single day, but it's not in the cards for me. "I'll pass. Plus, I have to help at the lumber yard when I leave here."

When my dad died, he left the business to my mom until I turned of age. My dad had a staff that had been with him for years, and I didn't want to take that away from them. So, I help when needed.

"Maybe another time." He punches out a text to Aubrey.

"Yeah, maybe another time..." I trail off, trying to push back the thoughts of what could have been.

Chapter 4

NINA

"Niki, do you think we could skip lunch and just head home?" I hurry past her to stop her from going in. "I'm just not feeling it."

"Not a chance. You've been *not feeling it* for three weeks." Her face softens a touch, eyes filled with worry.

"I'm fine. I promise. I just..." How do I tell her that what I saw today bothered me? "I need time. Okay?"

"How can you say that? You've had three weeks." She reaches around me and grabs the door. "You are going to walk in there and eat one of the best damn lunches you have had in a long time."

"Okay, fine." I walk past her and into one of the most unique bars I have ever seen. It's a modern take on your local, everyday bar. From the outside, you can see two levels, but when I get inside I see there's also a basement that houses a stage and dance floor.

"Pretty amazing, isn't it?" A blonde wearing a tight black dress walks up. "Hi, I'm Cindy." She holds out her hand. "I'm the lead bartender."

Taking her hand, I give it a little shake. "I'm Nina, Niki's sister."

"I gathered. You two look almost identical."

"How big is this place?" I walk over to the stairs, which are marked "VIP."

"It's crazy huge. That top section is the VIP area." She walks over to the ropes. "Wanna see the spotlights?"

"Niki told me about those." I look over my shoulder and see her and Gavin watching me. Taking that as my cue, I point over to them. "Looks like they are waiting on me. Maybe some other time."

"Nice to meet you, Nina."

We both smile, then she heads to the bar and I find Niki and Gavin.

"How do you like the place?" Gavin gets up to pull a chair out, waiting for me to take a seat before he sits back down, pulling Niki's chair closer to him.

"If you want to be that close, maybe you should invest in benches?" She giggles as he places a soft kiss on her neck.

"Done." He snakes his hand through her long, dark hair, bringing her head closer, giving her a tender kiss on the top on her hairline before releasing her. A sigh escapes her parted lips.

I had that once.

A whisper of a touch, causing your skin to prickle. Words that melted your soul. A stare so intense you could see forever within it.

I guess that's why I stayed with Brandon longer than I should have, waiting for the guy I fell in love with to return. I thought if I could just be *enough*, he would change.

Lies.

He is who he is and nothing was ever going to change. All

the signs were there. His touch, demanding. Words, controlling. Gaze, suspicious.

"Nina?" Niki reaches across the table, placing a hand over mine. "You okay?"

"Yeah. Sorry. I was just thinking about what I was going to eat." I give them both a wide smile. "The food smells delicious." I hold the menu up to hide the tears that threaten to fall.

Seeing them...that's how it should be. Protective, not possessive.

"Hey Gavin?" I hear Cindy behind me. "Jake's on the phone. He said he needs to speak to you."

"Can I call him back after lunch?" Gavin seems concerned, but as much as I want to look over the menu at him, I keep to myself.

"I don't think so. He seems off. You better talk to him."

She leaves, the clicking of her heels fading.

"It's fine. Just make sure he's okay."

"Go ahead and order. I'll join you as soon as I can." Gavin quickly gets up, scooting his chair back, scraping it against the floor.

I wince.

"Nina, you can stop pretending to look at the menu now." I see her fingers over the top before the menu disappears.

"What do you want me to say?" I lean forward and look around. "That my boyfriend beat my ass one too many times and I thought if I stayed he would kill me? Cause I think that's pretty obvious."

"Nina...that's not what I meant and you know it." She's the one looking around now, but apparently, it's still early enough that the lunch crowd hasn't made it in yet.

"I *don't* know."

I do.

She wants to know how I'm doing. If I'm thinking about going back, because that's what women like me do, right? Go back to try and save them. Been there and done that. *I tried.* Over and over and over again.

Feeling a little irritated, I huff out my acceptance that we aren't leaving until my big sis has some answers. "How about you ask me questions and I'll answer what I can?"

"How long?"

"It's kind of hard to tell..." I try to recall the moment I realized things changed, but it was so gradual, it's difficult to pinpoint. "But I guess when he suggested I drop out of nursing school. About a year after we were together."

"I thought you decided it wasn't for you?"

"Well, it really wasn't. I guess that's why I thought, '*Why not?*'" The memory is so vivid. Life changing. Step one of stripping me of my independence.

"*Nina, I was thinking. You know how you said you weren't sure that nursing was for you?*" *Brandon says as he walks out of the bathroom, towel wrapped around his waist.*

"*Uh, yeah?*" *I lick my lips and watch the droplets fall from his hair, down his face and along his abs before they reach the top of the white cotton towel.*

"*Eyes up here, doll.*" *His smile is wicked.* "*I was thinking, why do something you don't like? It's just wasting money that we don't have.*"

"*I wouldn't call getting an education wasting—*"

"*It is if you are taking money from* my *education.*" *He heads over to the dresser, pulling it open, grabbing one of his many white*

Love Conquer

V-neck T-shirts, pulling it over his head. "How about you quit? Stay home. That way you can spend more time with me." He winks and once again, I'm lost.

"Time is good." I sit down on the bed, taking in the view of him in the dark denim Levis he's now wearing.

"Very good." He turns and stalks toward me. A predator, ready to devour his prey. Slowly he begins to crawl on top of me. Inch by inch my body shivers from the way his skin grazes mine. "We could be doing this. In all my spare time." He leans down, taking my lips in his.

"I like that idea."

Biting my lip, drawing blood, he raises his head. "Good. Now I don't have to worry about those guys in your class." He bends to lick the blood that bubbles up.

I shake my head. "What?"

"Come on. You know what I'm talking about. Those guys, especially that one who is always texting you."

"Ryan? He texted me once about our study group." I prop myself up on my elbows, wanting to talk this out, figure what is really wrong.

"He wants you, but it's not a big deal. You're mine and now, I'll get you all the time…"

"Can you just give me a minute?" I reach for a glass of water, and take a sip.

"Yeah, but I do have something to confess." She mirrors my action, then placing her glass back down, she continues. "Brandon called the next day."

"Niki! Don't you think that is something you should tell me? What if…" I begin to panic. What if he comes here?

"Don't worry. Gavin took care of it. He—"

39

"What do you mean he took care of it?" I start to get up.

"Sit down and let me finish." She also stands, ready to tackle or hug me. I'm not in the mood for either one. "He called crying, saying that it was an accident, begging to see you."

"You told him I was here? I mean he knows you live here, but he thinks you still live in your house, not with Gavin."

"Oh God, no! I told him you applied for an interior design scholarship out west. He begged to know where, but Gavin took the phone from me and threatened him within an inch of his life if he ever decided to track you down."

I'm not sure what to say. Do I thank them for lying? For protecting me? What is the etiquette on this type of situation?

"So, he has no clue that I came here?" I begin to feel at ease for the first time in three weeks.

"Nope."

"Good."

"You guys haven't ordered?" Gavin says, taking a seat by his fiancée.

Niki leans in, instantly putting a hand on his knee. "We were just chit-chatting."

"Oh good!" He directs his attention to me. "So, what do you think? Ready to take on the challenge of making my house our home?"

"What?"

"I didn't get a chance to ask." She looks between the both of us. "But, we were wondering if you would like to redecorate our house." She folds her hands together. "Please?"

"I-I don't know."

"Just say yes! We need your help fusing our tastes together."

"I guess I could draw up some ideas tonight and work on it

Love Conquer

after work..." I mentally do a check list of the supplies I'll need. *Sketch pad, colored pencils, color wheel...*

"Gavin, do you have a measuring tape and basic tools?"

"Don't I look like a guy that has tools?" He sits up straight, puffing out his chest.

"Dude, you are one hair product away from being metro and you drink margaritas. Can you see where she might question your masculinity?" Niki is amused by her own joke; I'm pretty sure she just snorted.

"I'll show you *masculinity* tonight." He reaches over, tickling her sides, causing Niki to flail around in her seat.

"Stop! Okay..." She gasps for breath. "He is a regular Tim the Tool Man Taylor."

"I get it. He has a tool box." I smile. Their interaction is a welcomed distraction.

"A *big* one!" He winks, clicking his tongue. "*Huge!*" He holds out his arms.

Hiding my head in my hands, I smile. This feels nice. *Normal.*

Chapter 5

KYLE

WALKING THROUGH THE PARKING LOT and into Woody's, the lumber yard named after my father, I mentally make a list of the supplies I need. Working on the cabin this evening wasn't part of the plan, but after the invite from Drew, I needed an excuse to decline.

Heading to the back, I hear a familiar voice. "Hey son."

Looking up, I see my stepdad taking inventory, wearing his hardhat of course. My mom would have his head if he didn't. "Hey Jimmy. I didn't know you were working tonight."

"The truck broke down, all special orders expected today will be delayed till...tomorrow." He climbs down. "Or was it Thursday?" He reaches for the tablet he insisted we get to make inventory tracking easier. "Yep, Thursday."

"That works." I look around, not really knowing what to say. Jimmy has always been there for me and my mom since they started dating. When he married her, he accepted me as his own. So, when he lost his job as an investment banker five years ago, hiring him seemed like the right thing to do. At fifty-five, he was pretty well set from making smart investments, but he needed to feel like he was providing. Which I understand. So, I gave him a job doing something he would be great at: working with numbers and special orders.

"Are you coming to the big 6-0?" He rolls his eyes, causing me to crack up a little. As much as he likes to pretend he hates my mom's parties, he secretly loves them. Especially birthday parties.

"Yeah, Jimmy. I'll be there." I pull my phone out and pretend to check my emails.

"Good. Good." He nods.

"Well, I better check in with the office, then I'm going to grab a few gallons of primer."

"Be careful, son. It's supposed to rain and those roads can get pretty slick."

"Always." I nod as I make my way back out front and toward the paint counter.

"What's happenin' my man?" Dillion, a college student who runs the paint department while he is home during the summers, throws up his hand. "What? Going to leave me hangin'?"

Reaching up, I pat him on the back. "Just have to grab a few things and then I'm out."

"Here I thought I was going to get a break for dinner." He plops down in a chair, grabbing a bag of chips out from the drawer beside him, eating a handful at a time. Chip crumbs fall around him.

"Who's covering for you?" I cross my arms, sitting on the counter. Either someone called in or this kid is trying to scam another break.

"Normally Carl, but he's on vacation. He wasn't going to take it knowing we were shorthanded, but I told him I would just bring something in. No big deal." Another handful of chips.

"You know what? I got this, go have dinner. Take an hour if you want."

"Really?" He stands up, wiping his hand on his jeans.

"I have stuff I need to get done anyway."

"Sir? Do you have just a light gray?" an older woman calls over from the samples.

"You got this." He slaps me on the back, as he runs off, probably leaving a grease mark from the chips on my shirt.

Plastering on my biggest smile, I head over to the woman. "Hey there beautiful, do you happen to have an example of this gray?"

"Well, aren't you a sweetie," she replies. "I do..." She rummages through her purse, digging out a picture. "But everything I hold up to it either looks really blue or really green." She huffs, clearly worn out from trying to decide on a color, and hands over the picture.

"Ahh! You want this color right here." I pull out a sample and compare.

"Yes! That's the one."

"Good. How many gallons do you need?"

"That's a good question." She starts explaining how big her room is, using her hands and the size of my department. She goes on and on about what color it was painted before and the time before that and the time before that.

I try to find an opportunity to cut in, but my eyes drift to the opposite side of the department. The beautiful brunette from the coffee shop is here, in my store, looking at paint samples.

"Sweetie?" The older lady startles me.

"Uh, yeah...one gallon will be plenty. If you use this brand over here." I smile again and walk down the aisle, grabbing a can. "This is a primer and paint in one. It will cover the existing color and all the layers before that." I wink.

"So, you *were* paying attention, because I could have sworn you were looking at that little darling over there." She points.

I push her hand down. "Shhh. She may hear you."

"You *were*."

"No. Yes. I don't know." I begin to get flustered.

"Well isn't that just darling. I don't believe I've ever seen a man of your stature get this embarrassed over ogling a girl." She sets the picture and sample down. "I'm just going to grab a few things and supplies. Be back in a few." She leans in and whispers. "Good luck."

What just happened?

"I wasn't ogling!" I say loudly, causing coffee girl, a.k.a. Niki's sister, to turn in my direction.

"I wasn't," I plead.

Eyes wide, mouth agape, she turns back around and resumes fiddling with samples, picking one up and placing it back where it belongs.

Did I just get ignored? "I mean I was looking, but I wasn't ogling." I take the can of base paint and begin to tint it.

This time she shoots me an irritated look as she turns, but she still doesn't speak.

"Oh wait. That didn't come out right." I hurry and put the paint in the shaker. "I just meant I was..." Her back is to me before I can finish. "Noticing you were the girl from today," I say to no one.

As the paint mixes, I stand and wait for her to turn again, but she doesn't. I get a little side glance, but once she notices me watching, she turns away. Maybe she will need some paint. Eyeballing the time, I realize Dillion should be back any minute.

"Paint done?" The older lady is back with a cart full of supplies.

"Perfect timing." I walk around the counter, grabbing a wooden paint stick and opener as I lift the paint into her cart.

"Did you go talk to her?" Her voice travels loud enough for Niki's sister to hear, causing her to let out a soft giggle.

"No." I tilt my head to the heavens and beg for a do-over.

"Well, what are you waiting for?" She tries to maneuver the cart, but a wheel sticks.

Picking the front up and giving it a little kick, I set it back down. "For some privacy."

"Ahhh! Well, you go get 'em tiger." She makes a clawing motion with her hand and roars.

"Seriously?" I mutter as she wheels away.

"Hey, man. Thanks for covering." Dillion walks back in, soda in hand.

"No problem." I hand him a list. "I have to take care of some things. Can you have one of the stock hands get this order together and meet me up front?"

"Sure thing, man."

"Thanks."

Picking my phone up off the counter, I stick it in my front pocket and head over to coffee girl.

"What I was trying to say..." I begin to clear up the situation earlier, but look down to see her putting all the paint samples in the right places. Not looking at the names, just putting them back by a quick once-over glance. "Why you are doing that?"

Love Conquer

She twists to look at me, holding a handful of samples. "I don't know."

Reaching for the samples, I say, "You don't have to do that."

"No, these are mine. I'm helping my sister redecorate." She takes a step back.

Am I making her uncomfortable? After what just happened, I'm the one who should be embarrassed.

"Interesting." I stand, hands in pockets, rocking back and forth.

Something about this girl makes me want to reach out and touch her, and her reaction is telling me she would like anything but.

"What? You don't think I can do it?" She folds her arms, challenging me.

"There you are. Now I can tell you are Niki's sister." I flash her a smile.

"What's that supposed to mean, and how did you know she's my sister?"

"Whoa..." I hold my hands in the air. "How about we start over. Obviously, you are taking this all wrong." I reach my hand out. "I'm Kyle. Kyle Lewis."

I stretch my hand out a little further, and she finally takes it. "I'm Nina Sanders." And quickly lets go.

"Nice to meet you, and just to clear things up, I *was* staring but I wasn't ogling. Not that you aren't ogle-worthy because you are more than."

"Oh."

The way she responds irritates me a little. This girl, woman, is too cute and sexy as hell. Her hair dark and long, body slim, and her eyes...they are a green I've never seen before. I'm going to have to investigate them later.

Later?

"I was just shocked that you were here, in my store, looking at paint samples. That's all," I tell her, ignoring my thoughts. If Niki even had a suspicion I went there, she would start sharpening her knife now.

"Okay," she responds, blushing.

"Did you need me to mix some paint up for you?"

"Nope." She waves the samples in front of her. "I think I'm good."

"Need help finding anything else?" I try my damnedest to keep her here a little bit longer. Hell, I would show her every piece of inventory if it meant I could be near her.

"I'm good." She begins to walk backward with the cutest smile on her face. One edge higher than the other. Not quite a smirk, but not a full smile either. "I need to get going so I can draw up some sketches." She stuffs the samples into her back pocket.

"Let me walk you out."

"It's alright. You have work to do." She turns and when she does, she runs right into the end cap, knocking off a few boxes of nails.

"I'm so sorry," she says at the same time I let her know it's okay. Both bending down, we clash heads. "Crap."

She tries to stand up, but trips over a box behind her. Falling into my arms, she relaxes for a split second before she totally stiffens.

"I need to get going." She wiggles free.

"Nina, you okay?" I shove my hands in my back pockets. As much as I want to reach out and examine her from head to toe,

Love Conquers

I can tell my touch isn't welcome.

"Yeah, I'm good." She pivots and heads for the doors.

"Let me walk you out." I follow.

"No need. Front row." She waves as the automatic doors open and is in her car before they can close.

"Damn."

"What's wrong, son?" Jimmy comes up placing his hand on my back.

"Nothing." I lean away. This is one subject we will never talk about again. The last time, his help cost me the only woman I've ever loved.

NINA

I'M SITTING ON THE COUCH, which is now in the middle of the room so I can get a better feel for my canvas. My sketch pad on my lap and pencil in hand, a creative outburst flows from my imagination to my fingertips. Paint samples taped to pages, pillows flung all over the floor. To anyone else, it would look like a disaster, but to me...art.

I'm not sure how long I have been at this, but I'm guessing it's been a while. Once I got back from town, I was on edge from running into Mr. Tall Guy.

Kyle Lewis is everything that I would have wanted before. He is perfect. Dark hair, chiseled jaw and steel blue eyes that pierce right through to your core. The only problem? I had one of those before and I can't risk having one of those again.

I push him out of my mind with each room. Measuring, mentally rearranging, I fall into a routine, a therapy of sorts, and it feels so good.

"Nina! We have pizza." Niki comes barreling in.

"Oh good! Niki...look at this." I gather up all my ideas.

"What happened in here?" Gavin's eyes are wide. "I thought you were going to make it better, not worse." His smile gives him away.

"Chill. I'll put everything back before bed." *Oh crap! What time is it?* I look around the room, searching for a clock.

Niki notices my panic. "Ten. We just got off work."

"That's right. I almost forgot." I was so distracted by Kyle that I forgot Niki called the house phone to tell me how I needed to get a new cell phone because she had no way of reaching me to let me know she and Gavin had to stay late.

"Uh-huh...tomorrow we get you a phone," Niki mutters, following Gavin into the kitchen. "Meat lovers or veggie?" Niki weighs the box in each hand, teasing.

"Both, but while you guys are eating I have to show you this."

"You. Come with me." Gavin flashes his megawatt smile, letting me know it's okay. "Couch gets fixed now."

Niki and Gavin look at each other. "Couch cuddle time!"

"I'll grab the pizza and beer. You guys fix the couch."

"Whoa! I am not cuddling with you guys." I hold up my hands.

Not waiting on me, Gavin puts the couch back to where he had it.

"Of course not, Nina. You can sit over there and show us your designs." Niki sets the pizza on the coffee table and hands

Love Conquer

Gavin a beer. "You want one?"

Scrunching up my nose, I pass, trying to push back the memory of Brandon breathing on me after a long night out with his co-workers. "Entertaining clients" is what he called it.

"You guys get settled because sitting here is like a kid waiting to open presents on Christmas Day. Except, I feel more like Santa, not the kids." I start passing out the sketches. "Because I'm giving the gifts, not receiving. Well, I guess it would be my present since I love doing this. Oh my god, I'm rambling."

"Speaking of Christmas, remember that old record player mom had? Each Christmas she would play the Chipmunks' Christmas album." She trails off and starts singing, Gavin following behind.

"Niki!" I pick up one of the pillows, tossing it over her head to get her attention, but yet avoid an epic food disaster.

"I'm sorry! I'm just messing with you." She takes a long pull of her beer. "We're ready."

Her saying "we're ready" was like announcing a race. I was primed with design and rearing to go.

Ready. Set. Go.

Colors, lines, fabrics, I'm consumed and they listen to me go on and on until they can't keep their eyes open anymore. All of us head to bed and for once, I'm excited to start my new day. Not too thrilled about waking up at five a.m., but going in early means I get to get off early to work on the designs.

It's been so long since I have felt like this, was able to be creative and free. My imagination was my independence. Brandon used to encourage me when he thought it was a hobby, but the moment he thought I wanted to explore it, the excuses started coming in. I wasn't allowed to have an opinion or be good at anything that would cause me to be successful. So, this moment healed a little part of me.

Chapter 6

NINA

Today, I'm just Nina, an ordinary girl, waking up in the morning and heading to work. But first I'm going to be tired ordinary Nina, because let's face it, mornings suck. If I don't get some coffee stat, I'll be no good to the grouchy customers coming into Java Talk, looking for me to save their day. One. Cup. At. A. Time.

Grabbing my shoes, I tiptoe down the hall to the kitchen, careful to not wake up Niki and Gavin. Four-thirty in the morning is no joke and even though Niki has been greeting me every day at the butt-crack of dawn, desperate to get me out of my funk, I'm still more of a morning person than she is, and I loathe them. Which is why I head to the coffee pot first thing.

There's a note taped to the top of a freshly brewed pot. She must have set the timer. *Thank God.*

Nina,
Mornings suck, but I hope yours is great!
Enjoy!
N

Shaking my head, I open the cabinets, searching for a to-go

mug. Opening the door to the right, I see another note taped to a black ceramic mug that says #coffeesaveslives in white.

Hands off, bitch!

Reaching for the one next to it, I stop myself, realizing she meant this whole section is off limits. The mugs surrounding it all have amusing phrases on them.

Coffee Whore, cause I gotta have it every day.
COFFEE BEAUSE ANGER MANAGEMENT IS TOO EXPENSIVE.
I wish "you dumbass" was an appropriate way to end a work email.
A fun thing to do in the morning is not talk to me.

Deciding the shelf below is the safer bet, I grab a normal-looking, stainless steel cup and fill it, letting it cool while I take a seat and put my shoes on one at a time, because I'm ordinary Nina. Securing my hair, I grab my coffee and head for the door, grabbing Niki's keys on the way out.

As I get in and start the car, it dawns on me: I'm happy today. I'm excited to head to a job that I chose and wasn't chosen for me. I woke up for me, not because he needed me to find his keys because it was my fault they weren't where they were supposed to be. Today is the start of finding myself again.

Putting the car in reverse, I turn on the lights and begin to back out when I notice a bicycle leaning against the deepfreeze. It's the cutest thing I have ever seen and totally not Niki. It looks like it's out of the fifties, but with a face lift.

I pull back into the garage and get out of the car, an idea popping into my head. I take the keys inside and hurry back out to give the bike a once over. A rusted turquoise body, but sturdy

Love Conquer

enough to haul me around. Wheels, firm. A basket to hold my coffee and bag.

I'm doing this.

Walking it out of the garage, I climb on and test out the pedals in the driveway.

All good.

As I make one more circle around, I mentally calculate if I can make it before the coffee shop opens. I woke up thirty minutes early and I'm pretty sure the shop is only a few miles up the road. The longer I waste my time pedaling around the driveway, the later I will get to the shop. So, I go for it.

Nothing but me, my bike and the early morning streetlights. I can't help but think back to the night I left.

"What are you going to do, Nina?" Brandon is in my face again. So close I can feel the spit as he screams at the top of his lungs. "You going to leave?" He pushes me down on the couch, causing me to land on the laptop Niki bought me for school. I don't have to look to see if it broke. I could feel it.

He must have known too, by the look on my face.

"What's wrong?" He rolls me over with such force I fall to the floor. Seeing my laptop triggers another accusation. "This!" Brandon picks it up, shaking it in the air, the pressure of his grip cracking the case. "Is this how you applied for the job?" He throws it across the room, the impact causing the laptop to shatter and the drywall to crack.

"Brandon, I just thought—" I try to stand up, pushing myself up onto my knees.

"That's the problem, now, isn't it?" His foot connects to my chest, knocking the air from me. "You were trying to think, when I do the thinking for us!" he shouts, pacing. "I'm the provider! Me!"

"Brandon, I'm sorry, I just wanted to help," I plead.

I knew I shouldn't have said anything...my words are the ammunition he needed to lock and load.

Reaching down, he grabs the neck of my shirt.

Bang! Shots fired.

His fist slams into my face and I fall back.

"You did this. You wanted to start a war?" He falls on top of me, pinning my hands above my head with one hand as the other caresses the cheek now battered and bruised.

Leaning down, his lips rest on top of mine, his words just a whisper. "Nina, I love you." He lifts his head, searching my face for forgiveness.

Closing my eyes, I hide the tears threatening to escape. He's right. I did do this. I fell in love with a man who wasn't capable of loving me back.

He lowers himself to his forearms, both hands cradling my face. "Look at me, Nina. I want to see your beautiful face."

My beautiful, battered face.

I do as I'm told. Surrender.

"I told you I would take care of you. That I would find a way out of this mess."

"I know," I respond, waving a white flag.

"Then trust me."

"I will," I lie.

That night, I watched him shower and change. Going out once again to "entertain" potential clients on his own dime. Taking them to strip clubs and running a tab on his personal credit card. He thought if he just landed the right client he would make partner at the marketing firm he works for. In the meantime, he ran us into debt and blamed me for it all.

Love Conquer

  That night, I packed everything I could fit into two small bags and took the money I made from a few small jobs I'd done for the elderly neighbor next door. Brandon thought I was being kind and I was, but she was also paying me each month. With that and the change I collected around the house, I had enough to pay for a cab to take me to Niki's.
  That night, I powered down my phone, stuffed it in my bag and headed down the road.
  Vanishing.
  Today, I want to be *seen*.

Chapter 7

NINA

"So..." Jen glances over at me while wiping down the counter. "What do you think?"

"The morning was rough, but I think I did pretty well for my first day." I lean against the counter, trying to take the weight off my feet.

"Girl, you slayed it today." She spins around and throws the rag in the sink, but misses. She picks it up and smiles. "But you know what could use some improvement?"

I look at her questioningly, and she points down to my shoes. "Your matching game is off."

"Wh-what?" I glance down. "Oh my God! How did I not notice?"

"Navy, black, same difference, right? Plus, I would say your vision is impaired that early." She chuckles.

"At least they are both Converse."

"Word." Jen holds out her fist for a quick bump.

I would have never suspected Jen to be a fist bumper, but Jen is everything I thought she wasn't. Crazy, awkward, but cool as hell.

"Do you think you can handle it if I go on break?" She asks

Love Conquer

as she puts a slice of double chocolate loaf in the toaster, her decision apparently already made.

"Um, yeah?"

"Ding! Ding! Ding! Right answer." The timer goes off. "Plus, you can take yours after I get back." She grabs her loaf, heading to the breakroom.

Since there aren't any customers, I make sure everything is cleaned and begin to restock the supplies.

"Here!" Niki slams a box down on the counter.

I whirl around, startled. "What crawled up your butt?" I inch closer to the counter, curious as to what she has, but cautious as to what has her so irritated.

"I wake up today thinking, 'I wonder how Nina's day is going?' Only for Gavin to come in and tell me my car was still in the garage." She opens the box, removing a cell phone. "This, it's a phone." She reaches into her purse and pulls out a piece of paper. "And this, it's your number."

"Okay?"

"You are now the proud owner." She holds it out to me. "Now, take it."

"I don't want it."

"Don't make me hop over this counter, like I'm a star in the next Hollywood action blockbuster." Her hand-shakes the phone, demanding for me to take it.

"Niki, I don't need a phone. I'm doing just fine without one." I cross my arms, standing strong.

"Maybe *you* are, but *I* need you to have one." She lets out a big huff. "I freaked, okay?" She sets the phone down as I move closer. "When I saw my car in the garage and you were nowhere to be found. I freaked." She lowers her head, shaking it back and forth.

"Niki..."

Holding up her hand, she interrupts. "I was moments from calling 9-1-1 until Gavin noticed the bike was gone and called Java Talk. Luckily, Jen filled us in."

"I'm sorry, I didn't think."

I honestly didn't. I was so used to someone making the decisions for me, I got wrapped up in myself and, well, the rest is history.

"Just..." She scans the room before her eyes settle on mine. "Take the phone. If you are going to ride the bike, let me know so I don't worry. If...if anything happened to you, I would never be able to forgive myself."

A moment passes as we just stare at each other. I don't want to take it, but I don't want her to worry either.

"Give it here." I reach out, palm up, and she hands it over.

"It's a pay-as-you-go phone, but we bought you a ninety-day plan." She shows me some of the features. "I took it upon myself to program some numbers in there for you. Me being number one, for obvious reasons."

"Good to know."

"I also activated the location services and downloaded the app so I'll always know where you are," she throws in as she gathers up the bag and rest of the papers.

"Overkill, don't you think?" I try to make a joke, but the look in Niki's eyes is a cross between guilt and I'll cut a bitch, maybe both.

"How can you say that? When you showed up at my door..." She takes a deep breath and looks toward the ceiling, before she finishes. "I refuse to let that happen again."

Love Conquer

"Niki, there was no way for you to know..."

"The hell if there wasn't. You asked me for money. You had a broken ankle and you begged me to keep a secret about your school and savings." She holds out her hands, wide apart. "Big fucking clue."

"I convinced you everything was okay. I never gave you any reason to believe otherwise." I stretch my hand out to grab hers. "I love you for loving me, but I'm going to be okay and that is because of you." I pull her in for a hug over the counter and whisper, "Thank you for the phone. I'll always have it on."

She gives me a tight squeeze before she lets go. "Good. I made sure it was charged and here is an extra cord. Although I doubt your ride has a plug." She makes sure to get in the last word as she spins around and runs right into a brick wall of firm, rippled muscles — Mr. Tall Guy.

"Kyle, you shouldn't sneak up on people like that. What if I would have felt threatened and used some of my ninja moves on you?"

"I didn't sneak up. I opened the door and walked up to the counter. *You* ran into me." His dimpled smile is looking down on us both.

"You could have lost a ball." Niki looks down. "Or two." She steps around him and calls back over her shoulder, "Consider yourself warned, Lewis."

"If you're not afraid, you probably should be." I smile, letting him know I'm joking.

"Looks like you are in a good mood today."

Crap.

Last night I was so carried away working on sketches and then excited about today, I totally forgot about our run-in the day before.

"Oh-um-I...well..." I stutter.

The old me would back away, run and hide, waiting for the bad to come, but today is a new day and I'm moving on.

"It's been a good day." I return his smile, which has never left his face.

"First day?" He says as his hands go back into his pockets, something I noticed he did a lot yesterday.

"Yeah. That noticeable?" I cringe.

"Nah, I was just trying to make conversation."

"Conversation is good."

"Indeed." He rocks back and forth. His head turns, noticing someone coming through the door. "I'll be right back."

He heads for the door, stopping another guy, who is just a tad shorter than Kyle, from coming in.

That's weird.

"Who are we staring at?" Jen comes to stand by me, following my eyes. "Ohhhh...Kyle Lewis."

"You know him?" I twist to face her.

"Everyone knows Kyle Lewis, the nice guy no one wants."

"That's a joke, right? Just look at him." We both turn to see him standing at the counter, the other guy gone.

"Are we talking about me again?" His smile is a little more wicked than it was before. "Jen." He nods.

"Kyle...what can we get you today?"

Looking between the two, I begin to wonder if something has happened there. Did they used to date? Was it just a one-night stand gone wrong? Whatever it was, I couldn't help but feel a pang of jealousy in the pit of my stomach.

I know I shouldn't, given my history with Brandon. But I'm

Love Conquer

still a woman after all, and everything in me notices Mr. Tall Guy.

"Give me the same order as yesterday." A smile is still plastered on his face.

Does this guy ever *not* smile?

"Here, let's split the order, so you can go on break." Jen, writes down what he had yesterday and tears it in half.

"Deal." I nod and look back at Kyle, who is standing against the wall, legs crossed at the ankle, hands in pockets. Smiling at me.

Heat stirs within me, causing a blush to creep up.

Filling two of the orders, I place the cups in a carrier. "Jen, did these have whipped cream?"

"Yep, the mocha had extra." She nods over to a new case of whipped cream I didn't notice before. "I brought up a new case. We were out of the heavy whip."

"I have a little more in this one." I shake it a couple times before I aim the nozzle at the intended target.

"Dang it!" Air shoots out, spraying the coffee and whatever whipped cream was left into my face.

Hands still in his pockets, Kyle walks over as I stand staring at the cup, can in hand and cream on face.

"New can, Sanders, right over there." Jen snorts as she looks around the espresso machine, pointing to the box of new cans.

"Maybe I should have listened," I huff out as I look up. Kyle is now in front of me, eyes zoned in on my face.

"You have a little something right there." He takes his hand out of his pocket and points to my nose.

Grabbing a napkin, I clean off my face the best I can and return to topping off his drinks.

"You still have some, on your lip." He points to the spot on his face, but when I reach for my own, I dab all the wrong places. "No, right here." His hand is out now. "You mind?"

I shake my head. His thumb grazes my top lip, and he brings his thumb to his mouth, but instead of licking it off, he wipes it on his jeans. His hands go back into his pockets.

"Thanks." I stand in disbelief, curious as to why he stopped himself.

"Here you go." Jen walks up, saving us from another awkward moment. She stuffs the other two cups in the tray, then puts lids on mine. "That will be twenty-five, Lewis."

He hands Jen thirty and tells her to keep the change. "You going on break now?"

"Yeah."

"Can I buy you a drink?" He nods over to the booth as he picks up his order.

I'm not sure how to handle this. Maybe in a different time, I would have said yes, but now I have to focus on me, and having a drink with him will only make things more complicated.

Pulling out the phone that Niki got me, I hold it up. "I have to try and figure this thing out before Niki goes 'American Ninja Warrior' on my ass."

"Ahh. Okay, well maybe another time."

"Maybe." I begin to play with the phone. Just something, anything, to take my mind off him. "Dang it."

"What's wrong?" I look up and he's still here, staring at me.

If he wasn't so cute, I would consider him borderline stalkerish, but... "Stupid thing won't power up." I hit the button repeatedly. This is nothing like my other phone.

"Here let me." He takes the phone from me. "See." He turns

it to show me. "You just have to hold it down and to make a call you dial a number and hit the green button."

My hands fly to my hips. "Kyle."

"And to save that number as a contact, you just hit this button here and click add." He doesn't look up, but I can hear the smile in his voice. "Kyle 'look at him' Lewis, is that what you would program?"

Realizing he *is* doing this, I figure I might as well play along. "Actually, I would have put 'Mr. Tall Guy.'"

He gives me a side glance. "Mr. Tall Guy, huh?" He goes to work on the phone. "Alright, done." He hands the phone back. "Can you do that break now?"

"I don't have much of a choice, do I?" I retort.

"You *always* have a choice." His reply catches me off guard, making me consider his offer.

Finding the clock, I see I only have a few more minutes. "Ten minutes."

"Good. Do you want me to show you the timer features on your phone?" He points over to the booth he wants and lets me lead the way.

"Hardy-har, Lewis." Kyle stands waiting for me to slide in before he takes his seat across from me. The move reminds me of Gavin, always respectful.

"So, whatcha wanna talk about?" I wait for him to start us off. I'm fidgeting, so I fold up my hands and place them in my lap.

"Whatever you want to talk about." He fiddles with the tray, reminding me about his to-go order.

"Those coffees are getting cold."

"You want to talk about cold coffee?"

I shake my head no.

"They can heat it up." He doesn't seem concerned.

"Okay."

"So, tell me about you? How old, are you out of school for the summer or do you plan on staying?" He pumps out the questions, one right after the other.

"Twenty-three and I don't know," I admit.

"You don't know if you are in school or you don't know if you are staying?"

"School." I scan the room and notice Jen's eyes are locked on us. "Did you used to date Jen?" The words are out before I bring my attention back to him.

"No." He doesn't seem shocked or even upset that I asked. So, I press on.

"Then why is she keeping an eye on you?" I jab my thumb in her direction, and Kyle bursts out laughing, slapping the table, causing the coffee to shake.

"What?" I turn to see Jen shrugging her shoulders.

"She mimed that she was going to cut my throat." He mocks her threat. "But no, we never dated."

"You didn't?" I'm suddenly relieved.

"Nope." He shakes his head, slowly, back and forth. "I was going through something and leaned on her sister, Cindy. Things happened and..." I can tell the words are on the tip of his tongue. "It didn't end well."

"She hates you for screwing over her sister." I purse my lips. "I get that."

"No, it's actually the opposite. Jen and I get along fine, but I'm guessing she likes you and is afraid the same thing will happen to you."

"Will it?" I ask, daring him for an answer that I shouldn't desperately want.

The look on his face says I'm confusing him. I'm hot and cold. I'm drawn to him, but I know I'm no good right now. I have to deal with my hang ups before I even attempt a relationship, not that he is even asking for one.

Leaning forward, hands in his lap, he lowers his voice for only me to hear, "Nina, there is something about you. When you are near, I feel this pull toward you that I can't control."

"Kyle..." I beg him to stop, or am I pleading for him to go on?

"I can see you're not ready and honestly, I'm not sure if I have anything left to give."

"Oh."

"Nina, I'm not saying this the right way." He clears his throat, starting over. "I *want* to get to know you and I'm hoping you feel the same."

"So, you want to be friends?" I'm still not sure if this is what he is asking.

"Yeah! I can't believe I'm saying this, but I do."

"Okay then, friends."

Chapter 8

KYLE

Back on site, I don't even have to wait for Lee and the rest of the crew to come fetch their coffee. As soon as my truck hit the gravel they were lined up, hardhats on and hands out. "Greedy bastards," I mumble.

"What took you so long?" Lee walks around to the passenger side, opening the door and passing out the coffees one by one. He takes a pull of his, spitting it out immediately. "What the hell, boss? If I wanted cold coffee, I would have ordered an iced one."

"What part of free gives you the right to complain about your order?" Sliding my tool belt into place, I reach in the back and grab my hardhat. "Nothing?" I nod, ignoring their looks as I head to find Drew.

"Part of having a lead foreman is having the luxury to come in later because you know your shit will be taken care of." He stands at the white boards, examining, not even turning to acknowledge me.

"Sorry man, I ran into the coffee shop—"

"Lewis, what the hell? Do you have a death wish?" he interrupts, swinging around.

Love Conquer

Of course, this would get his attention. "It's not like I want to lose my balls, I want kids someday, if it's ever in the cards for me, but there is something about her." I pause, trying to find the words to express why my head is all over the place. "The pull is strong, man."

Putting the lid on the marker, he tucks it behind his ear and walks over to me, clasping a hand on my shoulder. "I get it," he reassures me with a little squeeze. "Trust me, I felt the exact same way about Aubrey, but if I can give you one piece of advice." He raises his hand between us, finger poking my chest. "Close the door on your past or it will haunt the fuck out of your future."

Drew and I have always been tight, but last summer he had no one to confide in when shit started going down during his divorce. We are talking about Pandora's box being ripped open.

His wife, Sarah, had cheated on him with her boss, which Drew walked in on, causing the divorce. And, as it turned out, her boss was Aubrey's ex. Their worlds were beyond connected, more than they could have ever expected. It affected their whole lives, bonding them all in a way they wished would disappear, but it was the hands they were dealt and each day is a learning experience.

I wish I could say the same for me. I was going through my own stuff during his shit storm. I was on a downward spiral and Drew was the only one I could turn to. Well, besides a few unexpected women sliding in and out of my bed.

At the time, I felt like I was the good guy no one wanted and being bad, it helped me forget, but that's the problem, right? Just because you forget, doesn't mean it's forgiven and I'm not sure I can forgive.

"Man, I'm working on it," I admit, thinking about Jimmy's sixtieth birthday party this weekend.

"Good," he gives me one last poke in the chest, "cause your head needs to be in the game or you're going to get hurt. Not only on the job, but in here." He slaps me on the chest and walks off.

I know.

"Don't forget about that lunch today," he tells me.

"Lunch?"

"Remember?" He's back at the white board, changing up today's game plan. "That couple I was telling you about, who hired that overpriced architect and designer from that TV show...well, we have a meeting with all of them. Today."

"Oh Lord." I roll my eyes. This should be interesting. These are the kind of clients who know little about what we do, but want to tell us exactly how to do it.

"Yep, and they asked that you take the lead on the project. So, I need you to be there and here." He points to his head. "Get in the game, man."

"I won't let you down."

Heading to Spotlight to meet with Drew and the potential clients, I crank the radio and try to get my mind off every distraction. It's working, until my phone begins to ring. Since I'm almost there, I contemplate declining the call but I see it's my mom.

I turn down the music and press the speaker button on the phone. "Hey mom!"

Love Conquer

"Hey honey." She pauses for a split second, which usually is her tell that something is wrong. "How's work?"

"It's fine." I drag out the words, curious as to what the small talk is about.

"That's good. That's *real* good."

"Mom, is something wrong? You seem...distracted."

"You know me so well." I can hear the worry in her voice. "I don't know how to say this, but Trinity is sick again, so your brother won't be able to make it to the party."

"Mom," I whisper. "Is she going to be okay?"

"Oh yeah, nothing like before. She just has an ear infection, but since she's miserable, they want to keep her home, in her own environment."

"Well, good. Not that she's sick, but that it's nothing major." I remember the party. "What about Jimmy's birthday? How about I take you both out to dinner or maybe you can come to the cabin and I can cook you both up a meal." The thought makes me excited. I was going to wait to show my mom the kitchen, but this is perfect. Just us in the cabin my dad designed before his death. "The kitchen is done and I can't wait to show you what I did with Dad's design. It looks—"

"Jack and Tristan invited us over to their house," she blurts out.

And just like that, my mood is ruined. "Well, maybe another time then."

"You were invited."

"Mom…"

"I know, honey. I just thought since things have been going better that maybe this could work out. I know Jimmy would love to have everyone together." She seems positive, hopeful.

"We made peace, but it's still hard." I'm referring to my relationship with Jack, my stepbrother. Our falling out was anything but graceful and our reunion was strained, but we do it, for our parents.

"I know..." she trails off.

"Mom, I have a business meeting in about," I glance at the dash, "five minutes. I'm going to have to let you go."

"Okay, honey. Be smart."

"Always. Love you," I reassure her.

"Love you, too. Please reconsider this weekend, or at least come down for a couple hours."

Not willing to fight this battle right now, I agree to think about it, press end and head into Spotlight to have myself one hell of a meal. Hopefully Cindy isn't in here.

NINA

Hopping off my bike as soon as I hit the driveway, I wheel it into the garage and head in to find Niki and Gavin cuddling on the couch, watching a new series they decided to binge on Netflix.

"Hey guys!"

I put my mug back in the cabinet, having washed it before I left Java Talk. I look over at them, lost in the show.

I dig my new phone out of my bag and shoot Niki a text.

I'm home.

Love Conquer

Hearing the ding she reaches for her phone, swipes, sees it's from me. Pushing up and off Gavin's chest causing him to grunt, she looks for me. "Smartass." Glaring she flips me off and settles back in.

Taking a seat at the island, I kick off my mismatched shoes one by one as I pull out my designs and begin to examine the room, trying to decide which one really works for them and their personalities. They gave me full rein to do whatever I want, so why not do something that is out of my norm, but totally them? Opting for something bold and vibrant, I go with the gray and white theme with a pop of Netflix Red, filling the room with pillows for comfort.

Seeing the credits are rolling, I know it's safe to approach. "Hey guys, do you think I can get your thoughts on these..." I hold up the winner, but instead of getting their input, I get soft breathing with a raspy snore.

This, right here, is what a relationship should be. There is so much love here and when they are sleeping, you can see the peace and comfort they find in each other. Getting an idea, I quickly tiptoe to the kitchen, grab my phone and snap a picture. I'll save this for something special.

Gavin's eyes open first, and seeing me standing here he smiles. "Hey."

"Hi."

"Hey, kid..." he reaches down, brushing Niki's hair to the side as he places a gentle kiss on her forehead. "Time to get up and get a move on it."

"Already?" Niki opens her eyes one at a time.

"Yep."

"You know how to ruin a girl's day." She sits up, stretching, not seeing me there.

"How's that? You get to work with me tonight!"

She purses her lips. "I guess."

He tackles her with tickles, and she falls back into the couch. As she twists around, trying to escape, she finally notices me.

"Stop!" She smacks his hands away. "Hey, sis."

"Hi. You guys going to be gone late tonight?" I decide to keep the design as much of a mystery as I can.

"Planning a party?" she winks.

"If you count painting a party, then it's going down." I laugh

"Ewe." She scrunches up her face. "Just make sure to get flat or satin. I don't want to see my reflection in that glossy shit."

She gets up, holding out her hand for Gavin. With her small frame, she's not able to pull him up, but still tries. "You need to lose some weight, Shaw." She digs her feet in, pulling harder.

Standing up, he lifts his shirt a little, showing that there is nothing to lose. "You think?' He places her hand on his rippled, washboard abs.

Forgoing words, she jumps into his arms and wraps her legs around his waist, kissing him deeply.

Feeling like a peeping tom, I walk over to the mantle and pretend to measure.

"Nina?" Niki yells from down the hall. "Credit card is in my purse. Get whatever you need." The door slams and giggles erupt.

Going to my room, I gather up a change of clothes and head for the shower, to wash the smell of coffee from my skin before I head to the lumber yard.

Maybe, I'll run into Mr. Tall Guy.

Chapter 9

KYLE

Lunch was a waste of time. The potential clients canceled, pissing off Drew — especially since he sent the crew home early. We contemplated going back and tag-teaming a couple small projects that need finishing, but thought why not have a couple beers and call it a day.

Lunch was great, but the beers were better. Lucky, for me, Cindy wasn't there to give me the stink eye. Honestly, I don't think she has ever forgiven me for "hitting and splitting" as she called it. Actually, I know she hasn't. Well, according to Jen, her sister, she hasn't.

In my defense, I thought we had an understanding. We both were going through something and neither of us wanted to talk about it. Hell, I wasn't even her first choice. The night we met, she slid Drew her number, not me. But, he saw Aubrey and was done. So, I got the napkin and eventually her attitude.

Being lonely is a bitch, especially when you had been with someone every day of your life since middle school.

"Go out and forget," they said.

So, I did. I just didn't expect for us to get stuck on repeat. For two weeks, Cindy and I met up here and there, but eventually it led to dinner after or drinks before. Which, to most women, means *we're dating*.

I didn't know!

After that, I threw myself into the cabin project, working nights and weekends to finally finish what my dad started. I just wish he could be here to see it.

Miss you, Dad.

Everywhere I turn, my dad is there. Woody's, the cabin, the craft I inherited. He lives on in me and the things I do. Someday I hope to pass on the things he taught me.

Turning into Woody's lot, I park my truck in back and wait for them to load up the materials I need to finish the deck.

"Hi, son." Jimmy comes strolling out, tablet in hand, updating inventory.

"Hey, Jimmy." I round the bed and lower the gate.

"Your mom said she talked to you..."

Holding up my hand, I stop him. "Jimmy, I'm trying hard to move on to make you guys happy, but it's difficult."

"I know son." He pats me on the back and I wince.

As much as I know he means the words, I can't help the jealousy that rears its ugly head. He chose his real son to spend his birthday with. Jack and his family. The family I wish I had.

"You know your mom just wants to get things back to the way they were," he says, as if it's that simple, as if saying the words will make everything go away and heal itself. It won't.

Pulling out the radio, he calls for the loaders to bring out the order and continues. "You guys talked it out like brothers should. It's about time we throw ourselves back together and make this family whole again."

"Jimmy, it's not that simple. You can't just patch this up and make it better." I run both hands through my hair. "I'm working on it, but it hurts," I admit.

"It will get easier the more we are around each other."

"I'm not the one who canceled," I bark at him.

"You could come —"

"I'm not going to *their* home," I interrupt.

"Okay, son. I get it, I do." He pulls me to the side as they begin to load. "That is why I invited Jack and Tristan to have Trinity's second birthday party at our house. Not theirs."

Two?

Pinching the bridge of my nose, I look on, unsure of what to say.

"Just say you will be there. It would make your mom happy."

What about my happiness?

"Just have Mom message me the date," I say, but I don't need the text. I know exactly when she was born. How can you ever forget a moment like that? Fourth of July fireworks, water breaking, a baby born in the back of your truck. Kind of unforgettable.

"Will do." His phone begins to ring. "I better get this."

Giving a little wave, I head inside to pick up a few things.

NINA

When life hands you lemons, you make lemonade or, in my case, a make-shift bike trailer. The one day I did need Niki's car is the one time she decides to take it. While I took my shower and changed into appropriate painting attire — tank top and yoga pants — Niki and Gavin left, taking both cars.

So, I went over my list to see what I could manage and still maneuver the bike. The basket could carry the supplies and if I got two cans of paint, I could balance them on top of everything, against the handlebars.

Perfect!

When I'm almost to the store, I notice something next to a dumpster — a little rusted wagon. I stop next to it, pull it out and wheel it around.

Seems fine.

Reaching into my basket, I pull out a couple bungee cords and attach the wagon to the back of the bike.

Score!

Throwing my hands in the air I do a little shimmy, not caring who's watching, to celebrate my little win. I did this. I came up with a plan and followed through. I didn't need to get approval, I didn't need to wait for help. I did this on my own.

Giving myself a big ol' pat on the back, I jump back on the bike and continue on my adventure.

My head a little higher, I pedal a little faster knowing whatever comes my way, I will figure it out.

I can do this.

I ride the bike up onto the sidewalk and lean it against the building. List in hand, I grab a cart and head toward the paint department, hoping Kyle is there working.

Empty.

Love Conquer

Looking around, I see a couple workers, none of them Mr. Tall Guy. I could ask for their help, but instead I take a little detour, grabbing all my other supplies first.

Making my rounds, I throw everything I need for the remodel into the cart. Paint brushes, tape, plastic, roller, extender, screws, nails, anything I can think of, I throw into the basket. With my new makeshift bike trailer, carrying this will be no problem.

Rounding the corner, I see Kyle is back and leaning against the counter, arms crossed, typing out a message on his phone while he waits.

My phone buzzes. Fishing it out of my bag, I expect to see a painting GIF from Niki, but instead it's from the man standing in front of me.

Kyle: Hey friend.

Smiling, I punch out a text back.

Me: Well, hey there. How did your meeting go?

When I look up I see him typing back.

Kyle: It got canceled. Now I'm left with nothing to do. Any ideas?

I'm a little confused. He's *at* work.

Me: There's always work. ;)
Kyle: Just got off.

Oh, that explains it.

Me: Too bad. I have some paint that needs to be mixed. I guess I'll have to get this hot guy at the counter to mix it up for me.

That gets his attention. His head flies up and he scans the department until his eyes land on mine.

"Hey you." He tucks his hands, along with his phone, back into his pockets. "You finally decided on a color?"

"Oddly enough, I think it may be the same gray as the lady from the other night."

"Well, let's see what we got." Kyle holds out his hand.

Phone in one hand, samples and list in the other, I try to pull out the right one, causing everything but the phone to flutter to the floor.

"I got it." He picks it all up, handing me everything but the list and sample. "Is this the one you want?" He flips it in his hand.

"Yep, I need two gallons, please," I say, shifting from foot to foot.

"I got you covered." He's around the counter, cans open and tinting before I realize he has the list.

Oh! My! God!

I see the list, face up on the counter. All he has to do is look down and see it. Inching to the counter, I reach out my hand, but before I can grab it, Kyle picks it up.

"Let's see..." He starts at the bottom and works his way up, grinning. "Do you need help with anything else?"

I shake my head back and forth, heat creeping up on my face. "Nope! I think I have it covered."

"Are you sure?" His brow arches, his eyes sparkle with amusement. "I don't believe you got your ogle in."

"I don't know what you're talking about." I try to snatch the list, but he's too quick.

"It says right here," he replies, turning the worn-out piece of

Love Conquer

paper around for me to see.

#1 - Ogle Mr. Tall Guy

So much for being friends. I wasn't even aware I was doing it, but when I saw Niki and Gavin on the couch after I had the run in with Kyle at Java Talk, it made my mind wander. Not all guys are like Brandon, and what if Kyle is one of the good ones...like Gavin.

Holding his hands out, he rounds the paint counter and turns in a circle. "Ogle away, Miss Sanders."

Covering my face, I'm ready to run.

"Come on, you're going to miss the grand finale," he goads, reaching for my hands and pushing them down from my face.

It's been a while since I have appreciated another man, besides Brandon Thompson. I wasn't allowed to even look in another direction, caging my heart in a prison cell, leaving room for only him.

I felt like I walked through life with blinders on. My senses stripped from me, unable to enjoy the taste of life and right now, I'm being teased, tempted, and boy do I want to taste.

"Shake what your momma gave ya." He sings while doing a little dance, lifting his white fitted tee, just enough for me to appreciate the way his jeans are slung low.

"You're nuts!" I throw my head back and let out a little howl, allowing myself to live in the moment.

"See?" He's right in front of me. "Friends ogling friends can feel good, right?"

"Boss, you should have rung the bell." The kid from the other night walks up, pointing to the back. "I was in the stockroom."

"Dillion, it wasn't a problem." He puts his arm around me,

"Nina here is my friend." I tense at his touch.

Somehow sensing he shouldn't have done that, without missing a beat he steps away, hands in pockets.

"The rest of your truck is loaded." He hands Kyle the keys. "Oh hey, I forgot. Drew called a little bit ago and needed a new box of tiles. Apparently, there was a case damaged upon delivery. Said to send it with you tomorrow, but I just threw it in there since you were here."

"Thanks, man." He pats Dillion on the shoulder and faces me. "Do you want to grab an early dinner?"

"What did he say?"

I scan the floor. All the employees working have orange vests on with a Woody Woodpecker logo on it. Kyle is in a white tee and blue jeans.

"What did who say?" He tilts his head to the side, brows furrowed.

"Wait...you-you don't work here?"

"Miss Sanders, he owns Woody's," Dillion chimes in.

Giving Dillion the evil eye, Kyle says, "Actually Woody's was my dad's, but I guess I technically own it." He scans the floor, nodding his head in appreciation, and continues. "I work for WilliamSon Construction as the lead foreman."

"Oh."

"Does that change things?" He bends at the knees, looking me in the eyes, seeing my confusion.

"I guess not. I just assumed."

"You know what they say about *assuming*..." Dillion interrupts and both our heads turn.

He backs up with his hands in the air. "Just sayin', man. Just sayin.'"

Love Conquer

"Dinner? How about it?" Kyle looks up through his lashes, silently pleading for me to say yes.

"I'm going to pass." I signal to the cart. "I have a lot to get done."

"Okay. Well, if you get bored later..." he pulls out his phone and mouths, "Text me."

"Alrighty, see you later." I wave, pushing my cart as fast as I can to get out of there.

Making it through the checkout in record time, I get my things and go.

Back there, something happened. I was carefree...no, *careless*. Allowing myself to feel an emotion other than fear left me unprotected, unaware.

Kyle really does seem like a nice guy, one that I would like to be friends with, maybe even get to know better, but so did Brandon and look where that left me.

Broken.

Taking the bags, I load them on my arm, leaving the cart inside and head for my bike. Noticing the wagon, I realize I never grabbed my paint.

Shit!

The bags cut into my circulation, but I can't leave them out here, so I turn around to head back inside, but before I hit the doors a huge, black Ford 250 rounds the corner and honks. As it pulls up, the window rolls down...

Kyle.

Holding up a can of paint, he says, "You forgot these."

"I was just going back in there to get those." I open his passenger side and grab the cans. "I only have a credit card. Can I pay you tomorrow?"

Waving me off, he puts the truck in park and climbs out. "Let me load those for you." He searches the parking lot. "Front row full?"

"I rode," I say, pointing to my bike.

"Seriously? From Niki's?" He seems more concerned than amused.

"Yeah. The ride is nice and on the way here, I found this wagon." I set the cans down in it and show him what I created. "It's the perfect little bike trailer." I do my best Vanna White pose.

Am I flirting?

Toning it down, I grab hold of the handle bars and throw a leg over the seat. "I guess I'll see you around?"

"Get in." He takes the bags out of the bike basket, throwing them in his truck. Then he reaches for the paint.

"Stop!" I jump off the bike. I grab the cans from him, the weight of the paint pulling my arms down, and they crash into the wagon. Then I grab the bags from the truck.

"Nina, this isn't safe." His hands are back in his pockets.

"It's a nice neighborhood." I wave my hand around. "Plus, it's still daylight...totally safe." I mount the bike, standing up to pedal to help build up speed.

"I meant the bike!" he yells after me, jogging. "It's not safe and you aren't wearing the proper safety equipment."

"See you around!"

"Damnit, Nina!" he shouts, but I don't look back.

Never look back.

Chapter 10

KYLE

I DON'T KNOW WHAT HAS this girl on edge, but whatever it is, it's turning her into one stubborn individual. She always seems to be trying to prove something.

Hell, the bike trailer, I admit, was pretty damn creative, but leaving like that without protection is downright absurd.

Safety first.

Running around to the driver's side of my truck, I climb in and buckle up, putting it into gear. "Shit!" The passenger door is still wide open. I try to reach over and close it, but the seatbelt locks. "Damnit!" Flinging it off, I put the truck in park, jump out, round the truck, slam the door shut and hurry back to get in. I repeat the first process and throw it into gear.

I follow the only path she could have taken back to Niki's, hoping and praying she is okay. I scan the road, but she's nowhere to be seen.

"There you are," I mutter when I finally catch a glimpse of her pedaling down the sidewalk.

Pulling over, I creep along the side of the road, next to the bike path, looking between her and possible oncoming bikers.

She looks like she has it all under control. Feisty and cute as hell, she trucks along on that old, rusted, retro bike fitted with a brown wicker basket stuffed with plastic bags full of paint supplies. And, of course, tugging that worn wagon along, which is wobbling from the shifting of the paint.

As irritated as I am, I roll down the window and pull out my phone to snap a picture.

"Kyle, I got this." She gives me a sideways glance. "Did you just take my picture?"

Shrugging my shoulders, I look ahead and see her path is clear. "Maybe."

"Delete it! Now!"

"I'll let you delete it if you get in."

Good one, Lewis. Blackmail.

"I'm practically home." She pedals a little harder.

"Most accidents occur just a few miles from home," I shoot back.

"Automobile accidents." She points to my truck. "That's you."

We continue on for a few moments in silence.

"Oh shit!" Nina hits an uneven piece of sidewalk, throwing her bike off balance. The cans shift to one side, causing the wagon to overturn, which takes the bike down, throwing her off.

Slamming on my brakes, I throw the truck in park, flip on my hazards, and run over to her. "Nina, are you okay?" I'm on my knees examining her from head to toe.

"Yeah, I was fine until you made me run off the road." She jabs me in the chest. "You were distracting me."

She stands up, righting her bike and dusting herself off.

"I was trying to *help* you."

Love Conquer

"Does this look like you helped?"

She straightens the wagon, but the wheels are bent. Unhooking the cords, she picks up the wagon and takes it to a nearby dumpster.

"Here, hold these." She hands me the paint cans before she mounts her bike. "I'll take that one." She grabs a pail from me and puts the handle over one handlebar then holds out her hand for the other.

"The hell if you are…" I notice the blood dripping down her arms.

"I am, now give it here."

"You're hurt." I pull my shirt over my head, ripping it in a couple pieces. "You're bleeding." I nod at her elbow. "Give it here."

Nina huffs out, "Fine, but only because I hate blood."

I tie a strip of shirt around it, applying pressure.

"Other one."

She holds out her other arm, but this one has a little more dirt and gravel in it. "Listen, I have a first aid kit in my truck, but since I'm blocking part of the road, why don't you get in and let me help you back at the house?"

"I'm fine." She stands up too quick and stumbles a little. Her eyes show her surrender and she sighs. "Okay, but just know I'm not going because I couldn't do this or I'm too weak."

"I never said that." I open the door for her, and help her up. Then I throw her bike into the bed of the truck and gather her supplies before I get in. "I just thought you should have worn a helmet."

Safety first.

NINA

One minute everything was fun and playful and the next...awkward.

Am I the one who made it that way?

Am I that screwed up I don't even know how to get to know someone anymore? Of course, I'm not going to know about his place of employment, because I didn't ask him. It's not a betrayal. He wasn't hiding it.

Turning toward Kyle, I see him. Really *see* him. He literally gave the shirt off his back for me. He was concerned for my safety. Not trying to harm me.

"Just because I had an accident doesn't mean I couldn't have done it myself," I blurt out, though I'm not sure why. Did I need to convince myself?

"I know." Kyle looks at me out of the corner of his eye, smiling.

"Okay. Good."

I sit and stare at him, or maybe it's examining. Yes, I'm going to call it that. Staring is kind of creepy. Examining is more observant.

His body is ripped, and his arms? If you would look up arm porn, I'm pretty sure there would be a picture of Kyle's biceps. Total perfection. His skin, kissed by the sun. His hands, calloused. This man screams hard worker. Mr. Tall Guy is not afraid to get down and dirty.

"If you keep looking at me like that, I'm going to think you may want to be more than friends." He winks.

"Wh-what?"

Oh my God. Was I...

"Eyes up here, Nina. Eyes up here." He glances at me then looks back to the road.

"I wasn't...Oh, for Pete's sake. I totally was, but not for—"

"It's okay...I liked it," he interrupts.

"I was just thinking you literally gave me the shirt off your back to bandage me up," I blurt out before what he said sinks in. "Wait...you liked it?"

"Yeah." He nods. "Remind me which one is Gavin's."

I slide off my seatbelt as we near, leaning over the console, pointing. "Right there, second one on the left."

"Seatbelt," he orders.

Eyes wide, I fall back into my seat. "What is it with you and safety?"

He pulls into the drive and puts the truck in park. He's still, hands in his lap. "My dad died from a blow to the head." He twists his body to look at me, a hand reaching out to check the makeshift bandages. "If he would have worn his hardhat, he would have survived."

"Kyle..."

"So, next time you get on that bike," he reaches down, clasping my knee, "make sure you protect that hard head of yours."

And just like that, I understand. He wasn't trying to tell me what to do. He wasn't insinuating I couldn't handle myself. He was watching out for me.

He cares.

Before I can reach for the handle, Kyle is there, opening the door, gesturing me out with an exaggerated swoop of his hand. "I'll grab the bags and first aid kit. You head to the bathroom."

"I'm fine, let me..."

He drops both hands to my waist and leans in, eyes searching mine. "Nina, it's okay to let people help you. Let *me* help you."

"You're naked." The words are out of my mouth before I can control them.

His eyes scrunch up as he examines himself. "Not naked, Nina."

"Well, your top half is." I wave my hands around frantically, but he doesn't move, hands still planted on my waist.

"I'm a guy."

"Obviously."

"Your ogling is making me feel uncomfortable." He winks.

"Oh Lord," I mutter, throwing my head back. "Fine." I secure my arms around his neck. Totally not necessary, but I tell myself it's for safety reasons. You know, because safety first. Kyle said so himself.

"Good." He lifts me out of my seat and gently sets me down. "You okay to walk?" His face is inches away from mine.

"Mmm-hmm."

Kyle reaches up and unclasps my hands and, holding them in his, drags them down his perfectly sculpted body. I'm mesmerized by the way each muscle flexes with his movement.

"You look a little flushed." I feel the sudden loss of his hands as they cradle my face, pushing back my hair, getting a better look. "Maybe I should carry you in?" His face, once serious, suddenly contorts with amusement.

Slapping my hands on his chest, I push him away. "I'm fine."

"Hey!" He feigns being wounded.

Love Conquer

"You're an ass!" I shout, throwing him the bird as I make my way up the drive. I hobble through the house to the bathroom.

"Moving a little slow I see." The deep rumble of Kyle's laugh vibrates through me. "A little jumpy, are we?" He points to the closet. "Washcloths?"

"Yeah, second shelf."

Placing the first aid kit under his arm, he grabs what he needs and follows me into the bathroom. "Now let's get you fixed up."

He sets everything down. Tucking his hands under my arms, he lifts me onto the counter.

"I think I may have scraped up my knees." I slowly pull up each leg of my yoga pants. "Yep."

"By the looks of you, I'm thinking next time, bubble wrap."

"Hardy-har." I stick out my tongue.

"You better put that thing away before..." He stops himself, an awkward silencing filling the room.

Eyes wide, I open my mouth just to close it again.

He goes first, "I didn't mean to suggest. I mean I did, but..."

"Bedroom. Closet. Shirt," is all I can get out.

"Huh?"

"Naked." I point at his chest.

"Ohhhh...sorry for the distraction." He puffs out his chest as he leaves the room.

Letting out a breath I didn't know I was holding, I turn around, look in the mirror, and smile. I *really* smile.

Kyle is making me feel something I didn't know if I would ever feel again, and that scares the hell out of me.

"It's okay," I whisper to my reflection. "Trust him."

"Trust who?" He's back, this time wearing one of Gavin's

black V-necks.

"Oh nothing." I hold out my arms for him to untie the bandages.

"I can honestly say, I never thought bondage would be my thing, but..."

"Kyle!"

"What? I thought it was safe to say with clothes on." He waggles his eyebrows. "Kidding."

That's the thing about Kyle Lewis, I have only known him for a couple days, but it seems like he already knows me. When I'm tense, he backs away. Uncomfortable, he cracks a joke. Stubborn, he lets me learn.

He lets me be *me*.

Chapter 11

NINA

"Gavin has a pretty nice place here." Kyle scans the room. "A little heavy on the bachelor décor, but still nice." He walks around the front rooms, taking it all in. "Cabinets are handcrafted. Amish, I believe."

"Really? How can you tell?" I take a step toward him.

"See this?" He points to the face of the cabinet. "This design is too intricate to be factory made. The wood..." He taps the door. "Solid."

"Why Amish?"

Kyle turns to me and smiles. "Well, I'm willing to bet, if I open this cabinet here—"

"Don't touch the mugs." I reach for his arm, pulling it back. "Those are Niki's. She takes her mugs seriously."

"Don't worry." He cracks a smile. "As I was saying—"

"Enter at your own risk."

"There will be a symbol or initials." He opens the door, "Yep, sTm, it's the same family who did mine."

"Interesting."

"I'm probably boring you." He walks around the room, running his hand along the drywall.

"Honestly, it's been a while since someone wanted to share anything with me. It's nice." I'm more open than I wanted to be.

Nodding his head, he takes in what I said. "So, tell me your design plans?"

"Seriously?" I grab onto the back of the couch, grounding myself. If he really wants to know, I'm liable to spring across this room and into his arms.

"Yeah...the gray paint...this room?"

"Let me just show you." I reach into my bag and pull out the design, handing it over.

"So, this wall here will be the shade darker." He turns around to face the fireplace.

"Yeah, I want this to be the focal point of the room. The other walls and the kitchen will be the lighter gray." I bounce over to the island and grab the brick sample board. "And I want to replace the marble on the fireplace with this brick."

"I see." He begins to laugh.

My face falls, his laughter taking me back to the time I tried to talk to Brandon about going back to school.

Tonight's a special night. Brandon finally got the promotion he has been working endless hours for and I got into design school.

Setting the last candle in place, I turn off the lights and take in the glow of the room. A vase of roses picked from the rose bush behind our house decorates the center of the table. Bowls full of spaghetti, Brandon's favorite, sit on each end.

Hearing the lock rattle, I fluff up my hair and grab the champagne.

"Nina, you in...Ohhhh." He stops in the middle of the kitchen, kicking the door shut with his foot. "Well hello there." He drops his briefcase and swoops me up in his arms and my legs instantly wrap

around him. "What's all this?"

"It's a 'my incredible boyfriend got a promotion' dinner, and I have some news of my own." I give his neck a little nuzzle and he stiffens.

"I didn't get the promotion." He pries my arms from around his neck and slides me down.

"No way! I thought you were a shoe-in and that tonight—"

"Well, you thought wrong." He begins to turn on the lights.

"You said—"

"Dammit!" He slams his keys on the table with enough force that it knocks the vase over, and the water goes everywhere.

"Brandon..." I hurry and pick up the bowls, but it's too late. The water has gotten into the pasta.

"Well, fuck." He grabs the bowls from me. "You made this for me?"

"Your favorite: half meat sauce, half salsa mixed in with the thin spaghetti." My smile is weak.

Dumping one bowl into the trash he examines the other. "I think this one is salvageable."

"Oh good." I walk over to the cabinet and reach in for another bowl for us to share.

Grabbing a fork, he begins to twist the pasta around it as he walks over to me. "Thanks, babe." He stuffs his mouth. "This is fucking good."

Welp, so much for that. I guess it's cereal for me. Filling my bowl with stale Lucky Charms is not what I call a celebratory dinner.

"So, what's your news?" Brandon sits in his chair and flips on Fox News.

"Well, remember how I redesigned our bedroom and you said

I had a real talent for decorating?"

"Yeah." He stuffs in another bite. "Can you pour me some of that bubbly stuff?" He points to his mouth. "Wash this down."

I set my bowl down, not feeling very hungry, and pop the champagne, wishing he would wait till I share my news and we really did have something to celebrate.

"Well, I helped, Mrs. Nance decorate her family room and her daughter who runs an interior design company said—"

"Who is Mrs. Nance?" he interrupts.

"Our next-door neighbor."

"The old lady you help?" He taps his fork against the bowl. "What is her name? Phyllis? Joyce?"

"Margaret."

"That's right." He takes another bite, and a little bit of sauce splashes on his tie. "Goddammit." He throws the bowl on the coffee table; it wobbles, but doesn't tip over. "I thought it had too much sauce." He loosens his tie and walks over to the trash, popping it open with his foot, and slams the tie in it. "My favorite fucking tie!

"Brandon!" I run over to the trash, dig out the tie and quickly run cold water over it, removing any sauce, and then dab Dawn dish soap on for any grease. "I used the exact amounts you like."

"Something was different." He walks over to the laundry room which is hidden in a closet in the kitchen. He snags a T-shirt from the bottom of a pile of clothes I just folded, and the rest of his clean shirts tumble to the floor.

At this point, I just want to forget I even brought anything up. Maybe he will forget I said anything.

"Okay, so finish...you helped the old lady." He lets out a little chuckle as he makes his way back to his chair.

"Well, yes, sort of." I take a seat beside him, on the arm.

Something I have done a million times. "She wanted to redecorate her family room. So, I helped her pick out some paints."

"That's nice." He pulls me down onto his lap. "Thanks for the spaghetti. I think the sauce was right. It was the grease. You didn't rinse the meat. That had to be it."

"Sorry."

"Continue." He turns me on his lap to face him, my legs on either side of his.

"Well, she loved it, but when her daughter came over, she was in awe." I'm practically bouncing with excitement now.

"Keep bouncing like that and I'll have to bend you over right here." He raises his hips at the same time as he slaps my ass.

"Anyways...she thought Mrs. Nance had hired a professional." I pause gauging his reaction, but he is looking past me and watching the news. "When she found out it was me, she asked if I had a degree or if I had any hands-on experience. Mrs. Nance wasn't sure so she gave her my number."

"That's nice, babe."

"Brandon, she's that one designer. You know, the one I watch on TV on the DIY network."

"Cool," he responds, not listening to a single word I say.

"Summer Collins is Mrs. Nance's daughter! Can you believe that? And the best part is, she said I could intern for her, but first I needed to take a few classes to get the basics down and learn the terminology." Placing a hand on his cheek, I look him in the eyes. "She got me into design school. Well, not a full semester, but a couple classes."

He pushes me off his lap and onto the floor as he stands up and begins to pace.

So much for not listening.

"What the fuck, Nina? You think because you painted someone's house that you can go on TV and do this for a living? It's slapping some color on a white-ass wall and saying you gave it a make-over."

"It's more than that," I tell him. *"I'm not going to work every day and bust my ass to pay for school for you to learn the color wheel."*

"But you loved how I decorated our bedroom." I stand up. "You said I had a real talent for it."

He begins to laugh, bending over at the waist. His laughter echoes throughout the room. "I wanted to get laid."

"Don't laugh at me." I stomp over to Kyle, snatching the sketch out of his hand.

"Hey, I was looking at that." He tries to snag it back, but quickly sees I'm not in a playful mood.

"I wasn't laughing at you." He tucks his hands in his pockets.

"Then what *were* you laughing at?" I demand.

I may have taken this shit with Brandon, but now I'm living for me and I refuse to have someone belittle my dreams.

"Nina..." His face softens. "What made me laugh was that you titled your design 'Netflix and Chill.'"

"Oh." I feel a heat travel from my head to my toes. I'm so embarrassed, and a little ashamed of how I overreacted.

"I'm sorry," he says quietly.

"No, I'm the one who should be sorry. It's just..." I trail off.

He's in front of me, bending his knees to get to eye level. He removes one hand from his pocket and lifts my chin, forcing me to look at him. "Your design is amazing. The attention you paid to details from the colors to textures, that is talent." His thumb begins to work circles on my bottom jaw, causing my body to go

Love Conquer

lax. "The question is, who are you hiring to do all this work?"

"I'm doing it." I reach up, gently pushing his hand away. "Tonight, I'm going to start painting."

"You have a lot of prep work to do—"

"I do realize what it's going to take." I step forward, interrupting.

"I know you do. I was just going to say, I'm not busy tonight and I can free-hand trim like no one's business." His smile is crooked, cautious.

"I got it covered. Spotlight has some band coming in tonight, so Niki and Gavin won't be home till late. So, I have plenty of time to knock this out." I walk around behind Kyle and begin to push him toward the door. "I appreciate your help today and thank you for bandaging me up, but I got this all under control."

"Alright, but if for some reason you get bored or take a break..." He holds up his phone. "Text me."

"Will do." We stand in the doorway, face to face.

"See you tomorrow." He leans down and gives me a quick peck on the cheek, turns and leaves.

Shutting the door, I rest my back against it, looking around. It's a lot of wall to cover and I could do it on my own, but why should I when I have someone *wanting* to help?

Pushing myself off the door, I turn and swing it open. Kyle is still there, unloading my bike. "Care to show me those mad trimming skills?"

Flashing me one hell of a smile, dimples front and center, he says, "Only if you're paying in pizza."

"Supreme?" I fold my hands together, pleading.

"It's the only way."

Chapter 12

NINA

I'm falling into a pretty normal routine. I get up at the butt crack of dawn and eat, drink, and breathe coffee until noon, then work on the house until late in the evening.

If it wasn't for Kyle, I would still be working on painting the accent wall, but with his magical trimming brush we were able to knock out most of it on day one and finish up the first coat last night.

"What has you grinning from ear to ear?" Jen sneaks up behind me, tugging on the back of my apron.

"Nothing really," I lie.

"Since we're slow, you wanna take your break now?" She grabs a rag and starts wiping down the machines.

"You go ahead. Kyle is stopping by in a few."

Resting my elbows on the counter, I scan the room. I catch myself doing it daily, but so far, nothing. She hasn't been back since. Maybe I made nothing into something, projecting my experience upon others.

"Oh?" Jen smacks me on the butt with the towel and rolls it up again for another strike.

"Don't you dare," I warn her.

Love Conquer

"Then tell me the truth. You and Kyle hooking up?" She jumps forward, taking a swipe as I scoot back.

"No! I promise." I hold up my hands. "He's just helping me do a little remodeling. That's it."

"So, why come in on your break?" She raises her eyebrows. "Hmm?"

"I told him I would buy him a coffee for all the hard work." Looking down, I fiddle with a string on my apron. "Really, it's not a big deal."

"Kyle and coffee, you don't say?" She reaches across me, grabbing a danish, her eyes challenging me.

"Just coffee."

"If you say so." She fills a cup with the filtered water. "I'm going to take a short break since I have to leave early today."

"Okay. I'll be right here..." I pick up the rag and start cleaning, "...wiping down the counter, working."

Backing up, she grabs an apple from the fruit bowl and takes a bite, her eyes never leaving mine.

She's right. It is something more, but what? We've admitted we are attracted to one another, flirted until it was inappropriate, but somehow, I'm stuck in the friend zone.

Am I ready? I guess that's the real question.

"Hey you," Kyle says as he comes up to the counter.

"Hey. Jen just went on break, but is only taking a couple minutes." I begin to make the coffee I promised him.

"Cool. Do you care if I sit up here until she gets back?" He lowers himself onto a stool.

"Looks like you already made yourself at home."

Winking, he pulls out his phone and punches out a message, before tucking it back in his pocket.

"I'm back!" Jen comes through the swinging doors. "Go, pay Kyle with *coffee*." She looks from me to him, giving him the stare down.

"Uh, thanks?" I untie my apron, grab our coffees and walk around to the seating area.

"This okay?" Kyle points to a table by the window. He pulls my chair out, waiting for me to take a seat before he sits.

"Here's your coffee I promised you." I slide his across the table as I take a sip of mine.

"Thanks." His smile is there, but weak enough his dimple doesn't show. "Were you still up when they got home?"

"I had just gotten out of the shower," I reply.

"Looks like I left too soon then." The dimple is back.

"You're crazy." I lower my head, hiding my face.

"Don't do that." He reaches across the table, lifting my chin. "Your smile makes me smile. Me putting it there makes my day."

"I don't know what to say."

"Just keep smiling."

And I do. Until I take another pull of my coffee and he still hasn't touched his.

Tilting my cup in his direction, I ask, "Aren't you going to drink yours?"

"Truth?"

"Truth."

"I don't even like coffee."

"Gasp!" I exclaim in mock horror, eyes wide, hands on chest, as if I feel faint.

"There are a million beverages beside coffee," he says.

"Then why come in every day and why not order something besides this delicious goodness?"

Leaning across the table, he pushes his cup toward me. "I drink tea. Lipton, not that fruity stuff they have here. Or water."

"So, that's why Jen was acting funny. She knew." I purse my lips together and look over my shoulder at her, shaking my head.

"What?" she mouths while shrugging her shoulders.

"I'm confused. Why even come in?"

He takes my hand in his. His calloused hands are rough, but his touch is soft. "I wanted to see you."

"Me?"

He nods. "Go to dinner with me tomorrow night?"

"Me?"

"You. I'll pick you up at six."

"Not coffee?"

"Hate coffee."

"Me?"

"You."

"Okay," I agree, smiling not just for him, but for myself, too.

"Okay." He lifts my hand and rubs his lips against my knuckles, placing a tender kiss on them. "Break's over."

Maybe, but we've just begun.

KYLE

THEY WERE RIGHT. MAYBE TIME does heal all wounds. Each day that passes it gets easier, but the days I see Nina, the dark thoughts slowly fade away, healing me.

I was a good guy, but somewhere down the road, I lost him. Nina makes me believe there's a reason to move on from the past and hope for a future.

Nina...she's definitely not your average girl. Behind those mesmerizing, emerald eyes, there's a pain. One that runs deep into the soul. I should know, I see the same thing in my reflection every day. The same look that screams to run the other way.

But today, I have a feeling things are about to change. After just four days, I have the need to know everything about her. I want to be the one who breaks down the walls so I can shield her with my armor.

This woman makes me want to look forward to tomorrow. Not just Saturday, but every tomorrow after that. Nina Sanders is more than just words. She could very well be the story I was waiting for to be written.

"Kyle Lewis, I swear if that pansy lookin' grin is for my sister, I'm going to—"

"Have my balls?" I look over my shoulder to give Niki my best *"I'd like to see you try it"* glare, but the look on her face causes my mine to drop. My future flashes before my eyes. *There's scrubs, a scalpel and rope. Lots of rope. Any hope to have a family of my own. Gone.*

"You wanna rethink that?" Niki's arms are crossed, toe tapping.

"Oh Lord!" Aubrey comes barreling through the Java Talk door. "I can't leave you alone for one second." She grabs hold of Niki's arm. "Hey, Kyle."

"Aubrey." I nod. "Where are the girls?" I wait for the little rugrats to come busting through any moment.

"They're with Drew," Aubrey says. "He thought it would be

Love Conquer

good to have some girl time before Clark comes." She pats her belly.

"Ah, that's right." Drew gave the crew an early weekend while the contract team came in to do the concrete work. Since I've been a little late each day, I volunteered to supervise, giving Drew a little extra time with his new family.

"So that means you should be at work. Not in here trying to sex up my sister," Niki chimes in.

Glancing up at the counter, I see Nina watching us, a look of worry on her face. Giving a small little wave, I let her know all is good, *or it will be.*

"I'm actually on my way to the site now. The cement truck was running behind." I walk to the waste bin to throw away the cup from the water Nina gave me after her break was over.

"See you tomorrow?" Aubrey replies in a sing-song voice.

"Tomorrow?" I stare at her, eyes wide, racking my brain with what could be going on the same time I'm supposed to be having date night, with Nina.

"He hasn't told you? Don't worry, he'll call later." Aubrey pivots, walking off, leaving me alone with *her.*

I take a step back, and she takes a step forward. For being so petite, Niki Sanders sure is a force to be reckoned with, but in this moment, right before she speaks, her face softens.

"Kyle, I'm not sure what your end game is here, but if you think you can treat her like you did Cindy..."

I throw my head back. "Cindy." I exhale her name with a deep sigh. "You have no clue when it comes to her. Cindy...that was a mutual decision." I rub my hands over my face, irritated that one mistake has haunted me for so long.

"Nina...she's broken, Kyle." Niki looks down, pinching the

bridge of her nose.

"Niki, what aren't you telling me?" I take a step closer, whispering, "What can I do?"

"I didn't know." She shakes her head. "You didn't see her."

"See what?"

"No...I can't. It's not my story to tell, but Kyle...she's not like the others."

Others?

"Niki, from the moment I ran into her, I knew she was different and I swear to you, I want nothing more than to piece what is broken back together."

"She smiles when she talks about you," Niki blurts out.

"Well..." Her confession catches me off guard. "Same here."

"I like her smile."

"Me too."

"You better keep it there." She narrows her eyes. "Or my original threat still stands." She pats my chest. "Good talk, Lewis. Good talk." As she turns, she hollers, "Jen, coffee me!"

Nina's head jerks up at the sound of her sister shouting across the room. Her eyes find mine. Pulling my phone out, I point to it, signaling I'm going to text her.

Nodding once, the tiniest smile escapes as she continues to work. Niki notices and looks back to me. "Thank you," she mouths.

What she doesn't realize is I'm the one who should be thankful.

Heading out, I tap out a quick message.

Me: I think she's warming up to me. TTYL.

Before I can slide it back into my pocket, I get a text from

Drew.

> Drew: I need some help with a surprise for the girls.

Here it comes.

> Me: Have a date.
> Drew: All day?
> Me: Not till 6.
> Drew: We'll be done.
> Drew: Nina?
> Me: Yeah.
> Drew: Niki is going to... (knife emoji)

Noticing the time, I head to the truck, my phone pinging like crazy as I walk.

> Drew: Oh God! Are you at Java Talk?
> Drew: Niki and Aubrey are there. RUN!
> Drew: Are you alive?
> Drew: I'm 10 seconds away from calling for backup.

Hopping into my truck, I catch up.

> Me: Dude...I was walking to truck, but it's cool...
> Me: We talked.
> Drew: I'm scared. I have a friend who knows a friend.
> Me: ?????
> Drew: Specializes in making people "disappear". You can start over.
> Me: Dude? Ye of little faith.
> Drew: LOL

Me: What time tomorrow?

Drew: After Doug gets the girls. Around 2-ish?

Me: What are we doing?

Drew: Moving a playhouse.

Me: I'll be there at noon.

Drew: Good. Girls are fixing lunch.

Me: Is this code for show up with a pizza.

Drew: I wish. Since learning to make tacos we have it every other day.

Me: LOL

Drew: I'll let you go. Buzz me when the job's done.

Me: 10-4

Tossing my phone in the console, I sit back and revel in my win. Tomorrow is a new day.

Chapter 13

NINA

"Rise and shine!" I run into Niki's room. "It's Saturday!" I yell, jumping up onto the bed with one of Niki's non-spill stainless steel mugs in hand.

"For fuck's sake." She pulls the cover over her head. "Why does everyone feel the need to pounce on me this morning?"

"Wha..." I stop jumping and fall into the bed.

Throwing back the covers, she says, "First Gav..." She nods over to where I landed, giving me a little wink. "And now you."

"Ew!" I scramble to get off the bed, but not before Niki snags the mug from my hands, downing the contents like it's a cold bottle of water.

"I'm kidding." She stretches out, blindly searching for the nightstand to set her cup down. "Gav stayed after closing to work with Jake on the quarterly inventory."

Crawling across the bed, I grab her mug and set it down.

"Thanks." She stretches out. "So, what has you up and going on your day off?" Niki reaches for Gavin's pillow, hugging it tight as she buries her nose in his scent.

"Well, I was wondering if you wanted to have a girl's day?" I wiggle my toes. "They are in desperate need of a pedicure."

"Oh hell no!"

"Why?"

"Pedicures mean shaven legs and shaven legs equals swinging chandelier sex."

"Niki!" I fall back on the bed. "You're unbelievable." I roll over, now facing her. "It means a touch of colors on my toes during flip-flop season."

"Which leads to sex."

"I'm twenty-three years old. If I want to have sex on the first date I will, but honestly, it's just dinner."

"Said no woman ever." She sits up, scooting back against the headboard. "We are programmed to have feelings, make mountains out of molehills. So, please." She folds her hands together, begging. "For the love of all things holy, please tell me, you did not let his snake, near your hole." Unclasping her hands, she reaches for the mug, shaking out the leftover droplets into her mouth.

"Did you seriously just beg for my celibacy?"

"Dear sister, I just prayed." She points to the heavens. "I got me some *God* on my side. Tempt that! I dare you."

"Cheese-N-Rice! You're unbelievable." I reach behind me, feeling around for my revenge.

"Nina...come here." She holds out her arms. "Come give your sister a hug."

Stretching out, I lean over, bringing the pillow with me... just in case.

Wrapping me in her arms, she whispers, "Don't think I didn't see that pillow."

"Wh-what?"

And before I know what's happening, her hands are on my

shorts, yanking them up, giving me the biggest wedgie.

"Niki!" I reach around, doing a little dance trying to save my lady bits.

Jumping out of bed, she grabs the pillow from my hand and hits me once. "Don't try to out dick the dickster."

"Dickster?"

"Prankster, but it sounds so much better saying, dick. Don't you think?" She hits me again.

"That is absurd and if you hit me again—" The feather pillow slams against my head. "That hurt!" I'm out of the bed in a flash and grab a throw pillow from the corner chaise. "This... it's sooooo firm."

"If you throw that and it breaks my chandelier..." She eyes the ceiling and my eyes follow.

"You don't?"

Opening the drawer, she begins pelting me with Gavin's rolled socks, one at a time. "Of course not."

A round of socks.

"That would take a special anchor."

More socks.

"You are unbelievable." I back away to the door. I'm raising the throw pillow above my head when it disappears. "Hey!" I swing around and see Gavin standing there looking exhausted, yet amused.

"I thought you two were going to have a girl's day." He walks past me, throwing the pillow back in the corner. When he gets to Niki, he wraps her up in his arms, inhaling her scent as if he needed a fix.

For a moment, their world stops moving. It's just the two of them, in a universe they created.

I want that.

I should turn away, but seeing my sister this happy gives me hope and right now, it's exactly what I need to hold on to.

After a tender kiss to her lips, Gavin face plants into the bed.

"Your kiss killed him," I joked.

Mumbling into the sheets, Gavin rolls over, propping himself up on his forearm. "What time is your appointment?"

"Eleven," Niki replies.

"Good. That gives you both time to pick up your mess before—"

"That was all her." Hands on hips, I interrupt.

"Figured as much." He looks down at his watch. "Yep, you..." He points his finger at Niki, turning it in a come-hither motion. "Come here. We have just enough time to cuddle before your girl's day."

Picking up the socks as she comes over to me, she says, "Looks like I'm being beckoned." She pushes me out the door. "Two hours. Me and you. Pedicures."

"Hey! I thought—"

With a gleam in her eye she says as if it was no big deal, "What? It's flip-flop season. Gotta look good!"

Then the door shuts in my face while I'm left standing wondering what in the hell happened. Oh, well. I'm getting my toes all cute.

Padding to the bathroom to take a shower, I catch a glimpse of myself in the mirror. I'm smiling.

Happiness.

Love Conquer

♡

KYLE

Walking up to the house, I can hear that it's pure chaos inside, but it's music to my ears. Especially after the phone call I just had.

Reaching the door, I raise my hand to knock, but the door flies open, catching me off guard.

"Kyle!" Andie and Reece jump into my arms and I have no choice but to catch them or tumble to the ground.

"Hey girls." I set them both down, rubbing their little heads. Waiting for their crazy-ass dog to attack or at the very least snag my bag, but he doesn't come. "Where's Putter?"

"Aubrey said he had to go back to Doug's house since the baby was coming, but we aren't supposed to talk about it because Reeses gets upset. Right Reece?" Andie glares. "Did you get it?" Holding out her hand.

"Yeah... Mom said we had to wait until we got to Dad's, but..." Reece chimes in. "Is it in the bag?" Reece's eyes light up while Andie opens it.

"Score!" Andie throws the sleeve of Andes mints to Reece and grabs the Reese's Peanut Butter Cups for herself. "What about the other?"

"I don't know why you need this..."

"It's for Clark." Reece grabs it from my hands and throws it to Andie to put it in a basket on the table.

"They think they need to buy a candy bar for their brother every time they get one." Drew walks up. "Lewis, I'm so glad you are here.

"My daddy says we can have a party when he comes home." Andie tears into her candy first.

"Mommy says he can't have them until he is..." Reece squints her eyes, counting on her fingers. "Mommy!" she shouts.

"Yes, baby girl?" Aubrey comes out of the kitchen, very pregnant and looking more tired than yesterday.

"When can Clark have candy again?" She unwraps a mint, stuffing it in her mouth.

"Not till he is old enough to chew." Aubrey tries to cross her arms, but her protruding belly gets in the way, so she puts her hands on her hips instead. "Baby girl are you eating candy?"

Reece chews and swallows quickly. "Noooo," she draws out as she throws Andie another mint.

Andie turns her back, hiding her face while she finishes her pack.

"Mmm-hmm." Aubrey waggles her finger at both of them, then directs her attention to me. "Consider yourself lucky they are going to Doug's. Girls, go wash your hands if you want to make tacos."

"I really don't know what I'm going to do with them." Drew shakes his head back and forth as he watches the events unfold.

"Well, at least they share." I clap him on the back and take a seat.

"True, man." He nods in agreement. "Hey, don't get comfortable. I need to show you something out in the garage."

"Is it our surprise?" Reece comes in first, drying her hands on her shirt.

"Shhh!" Andie holds a finger up to her lips. "Reeses, remember we aren't supposed to know about it. Right Daddy?"

Love Conquer

"Right munchkin," Drew agrees, turning to me. "They may be on to us." He lets out a laugh.

"Come on." He slides on his shoes and grabs the keys.

"I thought you said we were going out to the garage." I stand and follow.

"We are. I have to keep it locked so the girls or Aubrey don't come in." We head out the back.

Unlocking the door, he flips on the light and right in front of me is an organized disaster. Three projects going on at once.

"I may have over-extended myself this time." Drew walks around the playhouse. "This one is done." He shows me each section explaining we just have to carry the pieces out and secure them to each other.

"Seems easy enough." I step over to what looks like a cradle. "What's this?"

"Exactly what it looks like. It just needs a couple coats of stain and then sealed."

Then I examine the pile of wood pieces. "Please tell me you aren't about to ask me to build something?" I look over, pleading. "I have to meet Nina."

"Man, I know." He walks over to me. "But I'm running out of time." He takes the neck of his shirt and wipes his forehead. "We can knock this out before your date."

"Can't we do this tomorrow?"

"I promised Aubrey I would spend the day pampering her." He's practically begging now. "Man, we are used to having every other weekend together and now, with Clark coming, we'll have no alone time. At least, not for a while."

"The baby isn't due for—"

"What if he comes early? Do you see how big she is?" He

115

puffs out his belly, jumping when the Alexa announces a Drop In from in the house.

"Drew, Doug is running late."

"How late?" He looks over to me, worried.

"Between four and five."

"Shit," he exclaims, frustrated.

"Mommy? Did Drew just say *shit*?" Reece whispers.

"Reeses, my daddy wouldn't say *shit*. Would you Daddy?" Andie speaks up.

"Girls, fix the drinks!" Aubrey ignores their questions. Her voice is now muffled, closer to the speaker. "Tomorrow, Mr. Williams."

"It's a promise, Mrs. Williams." He smiles at the speaker waiting for the light to go off.

"Man..." I can tell panic is beginning to set in. "When you have a family, you will totally understand."

"Yeah."

"Shit. I didn't mean...I'm a dick. I meant with having a blended family like ours..."

"It's cool. I would be lucky if I had a family like yours." I bend down, looking at his organized piles. "Let's get started."

"I owe you one." He hands me the plans. "It's a simple design."

"Yes, *one day* you will."

Chapter 14

KYLE

"I THOUGHT YOU GUYS MIGHT be thirsty." Aubrey comes strolling outside, lemonade in hand.

Drew hops up and meets her halfway. "Thanks, baby."

"You're welcome." She stands on her tip-toes, giving him a quick peck. "It's getting late, I can order a pizza if you guys are hungry."

Stretching, I sit back on my feet and say, "We're almost done."

"Kyle found a few rough edges that I didn't catch. Put plastic edges on some and just sanding down the others." Kyle walks over, handing me a glass.

"Thanks, Aubrey." I hold up the lemonade before I down it.

"Are you sure you don't want to stay for pizza? If I call now, it will be here by seven..."

"Seven?" I stand quickly. "What time is it?" I reach for my phone and notice it's dead. "Dammit."

"Quarter after six." Aubrey looks between me and Kyle.

Drew's eyes go wide. "Shit, man. I'm so sorry. I lost track of time."

"I need a charger." I head toward the house.

"In the kitchen." He runs up beside me. "Look, it will be fine. She will totally understand."

"Man, I still have to shower and change clothes." I look down. "Look at me, I'm a sweaty mess."

"Shower here and wear something of mine." Drew takes my phone and plugs it in.

"What's going on?" Aubrey is behind us.

"He has a date with Nina...at six."

"Ohhhhhh!" Aubrey stands there while we both wait for some womanly advice, but nothing comes. "What?"

We both let out a chuckle.

"Any advice?" Drew asks.

"I got nothing."

With that, we hear a chime singling my phone is powering up.

"Thank God." I grab for it, pressing the home button, trying to make it go faster, but it doesn't work.

"I'll get the bathroom set up." Aubrey gives me a thumbs-up while she heads down the hall.

"And I'll find you something to wear." Drew follows behind her.

The phone finally lets me scroll through my contacts, and I select her number. It rings, then goes to voicemail.

Shit!

Needing to take a shower, I hurry and type out a text so at least she knows and isn't waiting on me.

Me: I'm running an hour behind. Had to help Drew.
Me: I'm sorry.

I set the phone down and hurry down the hall, but

something gets the better of me. I'm late and I sent a text. Running back, I punch out something quick.

> Me: Nina, I'm really excited for tonight.
> Me: Nervous too.
> Me: I just wanted to let you know.
> Me: OK now I'm borderline stalkerish.
> Me: See you soon.

Running back down the hall, I head to the bathroom.

"Thanks guys!" I yell out loud enough for them to hear me.

Stripping down, I turn on the water and hop in, washing the day's grime off.

Drew knocks. "You naked in here?"

Peaking my head around the curtain. "Come in. Almost done."

"Here's your clothes and a toothbrush." Drew walks in and sets everything on the counter.

"Thanks man." I close the curtain and rinse my hair.

"Oh, and she texted you back." I hear him set down the phone.

"What did she say?" I turn off the water and blindly reach for the towel.

"Here." Drew hands it to me. "She basically said it's cool, but I'll let you read it for yourself."

"Thanks man."

"No problem." He begins to leave. "I really appreciate your help today. Sorry it screwed everything up."

"Not your fault. I should have paid closer attention." I wrap the towel around my waist before I step out. "Now, let me get dressed so I'm not late for being late."

"Yeah, don't know if you could recover from that." He shuts the door, letting me get dressed in peace.

Black shirt and khaki shorts, not bad. I probably would have worn jeans, but it's a hot day, might as well be comfortable. I pull the shirt over my head and reach for the shorts. A pink pair of zebra print boxer briefs falls out.

"Very funny, Drew!" I holler.

After I'm dressed I quickly do my hair, opting for a slicked-back look. I search the cabinets for some cologne within the sea of glittered bath gels, but fail to find any.

Hurrying, I grab my phone and search for her messages.

Nina: It's fine. I'll be here.

Nina: I'm excited too and only a little nervous.

Nina: Confession, a lot nervous.

Nina: Be safe. ;)

Grabbing my clothes, I stuff them in the bag Drew left and head out the door, thanking them both once again for having me over.

Jogging out to my truck, I fumble with my keys.

"Get a grip, Lewis. You got this." I give myself a little pep talk.

Opening the door, I climb up, throwing the bag in the back and punch out one last message before I throw the phone in the console.

Me: I'm on my way.

Love Conquer

♡

NINA

I WAS IN THE BATHROOM checking my hair for the millionth time when I missed Kyle's call. I'm worried it's too boring or too big. Is my makeup too much or not enough? The back and forth on top of the excitement was giving me one huge case of the jitters.

When the doubt set in, I reminded myself of his words.

"I wanted to see you."

He didn't care that I smelled like coffee or looked like a hot mess, sporting a ponytail and barely-there makeup. He came in to see *me*.

Every.

Single.

Day.

That speaks volumes.

Sitting in the bay window, I keep my eyes on the driveway while I wait, unable to contain my nerves. I haven't gone on a date since my first one with Brandon. Which kind of started the same way, with him being an hour late.

The difference is, he didn't call and even though he paid for our meal at Applebee's I ended up paying in the end. He handed me his Oakley sunglasses to put in my purse, but I was worried they would get scratched up so I set them on the table. Where we both could see them.

After a couple hours of conversation, it was dark and neither of us noticed we didn't have the sunglasses, but the next day when he couldn't find them, he made me feel bad for not putting them up like he asked, so I bought him a new pair.

That should have been a huge clue, but I ignored it. We had so many amazing phone conversations that something so little seemed irrelevant.

Taking in a deep breath, I notice the time.

Seven.

Pushing the curtains back a little more, I see him coming around the corner. Jumping up, I run to the door and fling it open, skipping down the steps and to his truck.

"Hey! You're supposed to let me come to the door." He rounds the front of his truck, tucking in his black shirt as he approaches.

"I was excited." I bounce from foot to foot. "And a little nervous."

"Me too." He opens the passenger door for me. "You ready to go?"

"Heck yeah." My words are filled with awkward dorkiness, which causes him to flash me those dimples.

"Well, good." He helps me in. "I've been wanting to do this since the first day I saw you."

"You have?" I'm shocked by his confession. "I was a mess when I ran into you."

I wait for him to answer, but he just stands there, holding my door, and I can't help but think. Does he agree? I take a deep breath to calm my nerves.

Wait? Is that...perfume?

He must see the wheels turning because he chooses this moment to speak up, comforting me with his words. Making me feel a little less crazy.

Love Conquer

"You weren't a mess. Distracted maybe," he corrects me, "but a mess, not even close." He tilts his head to the side. "Can I hug you?"

"Huh?"

"A hug."

"Now?"

"Yep."

"Okaaaay." I lean over, opening my arms, curious as to where he is going with this.

"A real one." He lifts me up and out of the truck as if I don't weigh anything at all. "A hug has proven to help build trust and a sense of safety." He gives me another squeeze and I give in, relaxing in his arms. "Which then helps with communication."

"Mmm...I can see that," I mumble. "I like this kind of talking." I smile into his chest as he towers over me.

"It's the best," he agrees. "You know, it's also a proven fact if you hug eight times a day, it could keep the doctor away."

"Well, we are on our way to a living a longer life." I lean back, breaking the hug first.

"That we are." He lifts me back in. "Now, let's get out of here."

Kyle shuts the door and rounds the front, suddenly stopping when he gets to his door. Digging his phone out of his pocket, he stiffens, but answers, twisting from my view.

The problem with being in a broken relationship for so long is it ruins you for all possible fresh starts.

What was I thinking?

What if I'm just a fun time for him? Jen said he had a fling with her sister and it didn't end well. Am I the next one? Just another notch on the bed post?

Who's on the phone?

Whoever it is, it's causing Kyle to get upset. "Tristen, I told them I would be there. So, I'll be there." He begins to shout. "You have to realize..." His tone quickly changes. "Oh! Hey, Trinity. Yes, Paw-Paw's birthday is today..."

I can't take it anymore. Everything is making sense. Being late, tucking in the shirt, perfume and now a woman calling.

The walls are closing in, my throat begins to close up and my heart feels like it's pounding out of my chest.

I can't breathe.

I fumble with the door, push it open, and fall just as the memory crawls its way to the surface.

Standing in front of the mirror, I begin to twirl, catching my reflection in each pass. I feel so beautiful right now. Brandon paid for me to have a full day at the spa. Hours of being pampered was exactly what I needed.

This was his apology for overreacting a couple weeks ago when I accused him of cheating on me. I assumed when he came home after work, later than normal and reeking of cheap perfume, that he had been somewhere he shouldn't.

I questioned, he refused to answer.

I got in his face.

He headed to the bathroom to take a shower.

I knew I was right and the shower showed me everything I needed to know. I told him I had to leave, that if he wasn't going to talk to me, I was going to leave for the night.

Before I could pack my bag, he was on me. Pinned to the bed. Fingers digging in so deep veins popped, instantly purple, his nails drawing blood.

"There will never be anyone but you. You got it? You will

Love Conquer

never leave me! Not ever!"

I stayed and he showered.

Then last night, he came home and was so excited about landing a new client and when I suggested we celebrate he pulled out an envelope explaining he had been working on this for weeks. An apology.

Today, I can't wipe the smile off my face. It has been absolutely one of the most relaxing days ever and now, I'm standing here, twirling like a princess waiting for my prince to pick me up.

"Babe?" Brandon calls out.

"I'm in the bedroom."

"Plans changed a little, but it's still going to be great." He rounds the corner. "Holy shit!"

"I know! Today was the best! Thank you." I run toward him, wrapping my arms around his neck, breathing him in.

Perfume.

Feeling me tense, he pries my arms away. "The dress looks great." He spins me around "But why does your face look like a whore's?"

Running back to the mirror, I examine myself. "Brandon, it's just a little makeup."

He walks over to the dresser and grabs a tissue. "Take it off." He holds it out in front of me.

"You really don't like it?" My eyes begin to water.

Leaning over my shoulder we look at my reflection. He snakes one hand under my arm to cup my chin and smiles, applying enough pressure for my mouth to pop open in pain.

"Brandon," I plead.

"I think it was a fucking waste of my goddamn money." He takes the tissue in his other hand smearing the red across my cheek.

"Noooo." *My knees buckle, tears falling.*

Wrapping an arm around my waist he supports my weight. "You see this?"

I nod.

Black rimmed eyes, red smeared lips, stream of tears that left a path of destruction.

"I can't very well take you anywhere looking like that, now can I?"

"No," *I whimper.* "I can wash my face."

"Too late. I have Kate waiting in the car and you are making us late."

"Kate?"

"My new client." *Brandon lets me go, pushing me forward, right into the mirror.* "She wanted to celebrate with us. She wanted to meet you."

"I-I-didn't know." *I collapse to the floor.*

"That's the thing. You don't think. You just assume and then I'm the one always apologizing, picking up the pieces."

"I'm sorry." *Curling up, I bring my knees to my chest and bury my head in my new little black dress, thankful you can't see the makeup stains.*

"Now, I have to go out there and make up some sorry-ass excuse as to why you can't come." *He throws the tissue down.* "Don't wait up."

"Brandon, please."

He keeps going, leaving with the slam of a door.

Hurrying to the bathroom, I run the water and clean myself up. I need to wash the day away. Every single memory of its existence. Gone.

Without dinner, I head to bed. Curling into myself, I wait for him to come home, but that time doesn't come. Not until the next morning.

"Babe?" He climbs in behind me. "I'm sorry. I didn't mean for it to happen."

I roll over to face him. Not only to see him apologize, but so he can see the fingermarks that angrily kiss my face.

He runs a thumb along my skin, tracing the lines of my jaw, his eyes following its path. "Does it hurt?"

I nod.

Leaning in, he rubs his nose along my cheek until he reaches my ear, then whispers, "Do you smell her?"

I can't help it. My instinct is to take a deep breath. The cheap perfume is stronger than it was in days past, more intense than last night.

"You did this. If you would have been there, this wouldn't have happened." He climbs out of bed holding out his hand. "Let's shower."

"I don't want to." I bring my knees up to my chest, curling into a ball.

"We are. So you can wash her off me." He walks into the bathroom and starts the water, then comes back out and scoops me up in his arms. "It's the only way to move on."

"Oh shit!" I hear his footsteps before I see him.

Hurrying, I try to right myself so I can escape. I can't do this. I can't have this happen again.

"Are you okay?" He bends down, scooping me up.

"Pu-put me do-down." I hit his firm chest. "Now."

He gently sets me on my feet. "Nina—"

"I'm not going to be the other woman. I'm not going to let you go home and make excuses for why you weren't there." I start for the door.

"What are you talking about?" Kyle is in front of me, walking backwards, hands in pockets.

"You being late, the perfume in your truck, the phone call..." I push him out of my way. "Just let me go."

"Nina..." He steps aside, letting me pass. "I was at Drew's. When Doug, their other dad, didn't show, Drew ran them over there since Aubrey wasn't feeling good. My truck was behind their vehicles so he took it." He shouts out his explanation, causing me to stop in place.

"And the perfume?"

"Aubrey fell asleep while she was waiting on Doug to show and we were out putting together a playhouse. The girls got into her perfume."

"It's not making sense."

"Just stop and let me explain."

I turn and wait for him to speak. I want to listen and I really want to believe him.

He's not Brandon.

"The girls were drenched in all kinds of smells. The mixture made Aubrey sick and Drew wanted it out of the house so he took them over to Doug's instead of waiting for him to come." He's in front of me, begging for me to believe him.

He's not Brandon.

"Kyle, I'm broken." A tear begins to escape down my cheek.

I'm embarrassed and ashamed at the way I reacted. He hasn't done anything to make me believe he is anything but a nice guy.

"And I'm damaged." He cradles my face in his hands, thumbs wiping away the tears. "Maybe we can heal each other."

Love Conquer

He pulls me in, my head to his chest. "Hug it out?"
Laughing through the tears I say, "That makes two."
"So it does." He squeezes me a little tighter.
Looking up through my tear soaked lashes, "Safety first."
"Always."

Chapter 15

NINA

I HAVE TO BE THE worst date ever and truth be told, I probably shouldn't be going on one. It's been four weeks, since I left without a single goodbye and if I'm being honest, I'm a little worried about why he gave up so fast.

Why didn't he come looking for me? He spent years breaking me, locking me up in an invisible cell, for what? Just to let me go, no questions asked? The thought makes a chill run down my spine. How can someone go from not being able to live without you to being alone?

Maybe he isn't. Maybe he was thankful I finally left, freeing him of his demons. Maybe I'm the one who brought the worst out in him and he's replaced me. Finally, at peace.

Do I even care?

No, I don't. Two years ago, yes. One year ago I stayed, worried he would do something to himself. Four weeks ago, I left fearing what he would do to me.

Today, I'm trying to be me.

Who am I?

I'm so desperate to find my voice, to live my life for me, that I keep everyone at arm's length, terrified to let anyone in again.

Love Conquer

I don't want to be that person. I want to live life loving it, not second-guessing every person and every decision.

"Hey, you with me?" Kyle's voice is soft, concerned.

Flipping down the mirror, I examine myself. Eyes puffy and bloodshot. This is no good. Twisting in my seat, I frown, pointing at my face. "I can't go out looking like this."

"I think you look beautiful." His smile is crooked and kind.

"How can you say that?" I turn back to the mirror, tugging at the corners my eyes. "I look—"

"Like someone who just let me in a little."

Kyle reaches over the center console, holding out his hand, palm up. "Hand hug?" He gives me a sideward glance, wiggling his fingers.

Folding up the mirror, I give him my full attention. "You want me to hold your hand?"

"Well, I guess if you want to hold on a little longer than a hand hug is supposed to last..." His grin is back, dimples and all. "I wouldn't mind." He winks.

How can I resist that? He has seen all kinds of crazy in the last few days and each time I begin to push, he pulls. Not in a possessive, *you will be mine* kind of way, but an *I get it* one.

Reaching out, I intertwine my fingers with his, closing my eyes, accepting what he has to offer.

Understanding.

"See? Hand hugs are just as effective, don't you think?" He gives mine a little squeeze.

"They are." I'm lost in him, in this moment, forgetting the events that had taken place.

"Well, how I see it, since this makes three hugs, we can either part now, taking the chance we may need another soon, or we can make this one long, drawn-out hug. Soaking up all its superpowers, saving the others for later." He brings my hand up to his lips, kissing my knuckles.

"I'm thinking this hug has turned into handholding." I raise an eyebrow, curious.

Kyle's lips purse, his eyes squint into slits. "I can see where you get that, but I'm still saying hand hug." He nods, face relaxing.

I can't help it. I have a real smile on my face. Not the kind where it's forced, but a smile from being happy.

This man is sitting beside me doing everything he can to set me at ease. I accused him of so many things...but instead of pointing fingers as I have experienced time and time again, he's showing me that it's not that serious. Sometimes situations are just that. Situations. Nothing more and nothing less. You just deal and move on.

Is that what I'm finally doing? Moving on?

"So, even though I think you look gorgeous," he gives me another squeeze, "I'm thinking going out is not an option, am I right?"

Swinging my head around, I take him in, wondering what is the right answer. Before, I would have run every scenario in my head, contemplating the outcome.

Flipping the mirror back down, one handed, I look myself over. Eyes wide, yet clear. The puffiness almost gone. Makeup a little worn, but not noticeable. Honestly, we could go somewhere, but I'm not willing to leave this moment, the security of being safe.

"Do you care if we just get a pizza or maybe a sandwich to go?" I quickly turn, not wanting to see his reaction. I would

Love Conquer

hate myself if he was disappointed.

"Of course not. How about..." He trails off.

"Or we could drive around and I'll just eat something when I get back." I can't help but continue. "I mean that's if you want to drive around. I know this isn't what you had planned—"

"Nina..." Another squeeze. This one longer, putting me at ease.

Maybe this hugging thing is for real.

"I was just going to suggest something, but I don't want to freak you out or you to get the wrong idea." He brings our hands back up. This time brushing my knuckles over his lips, while he searches my face. "I want to take you someplace, but I want it to be a surprise."

"A surprise?"

"Yeah, but it's a couple miles out of town and, well..." Kyle takes a deep breath, setting our hands down, before he continues. "I need you to trust me."

Without thinking, I reach over with my other hand, placing it on his arm. "I can." I begin to lightly brush his arm. "I mean, I do. I trust you."

"Well, good." He glances down and grins.

"I'm sorry." I realize that I'm still caressing his arm. Pulling back one hand, I try to free up the other.

"I like it," he blurts out, not allowing our hand hug to break.

"I do too." I'm not sure where the honesty comes from.

"Then hands back on me, woman." He turns, taking us down a long, dark, and very rocky road. "Remember? Trust."

"I can do abandoned road, but if we pass a cemetery then I'm outta here," I laugh

Kyle stiffens, slowing down. "What about pets?"

"I love animals."

"Dead ones?"

"Okay this isn't exactly..." I search the area, wondering if I made the wrong decision.

"Pet cemetery. Just a small one," he says. "Actually, I'm not even sure if you can see it from the road." He looks over to me. "I promise, it's not as creepy as it sounds."

"Remember that movie?" I shiver thinking about it.

"Confession? I can't do scary movies. They freak me out." He lets out a slight laugh.

"Me too."

"It's the music."

"You totally get me. Sometimes, if something freaky comes on the TV, I'll throw my hands over my ears and sing *la-la-la-la* until it's over," I tell him.

"Well, I'm not that bad."

"So, I'm guessing you don't like Halloween either?" I ask, enjoying our little conversation.

"I love it, just not scary costumes. I think they're unnecessary."

"Christmas?"

"It's everything, especially the cookies."

"I make really awesome Christmas cookies."

"Can't wait to try some." He winks.

Christmas? Cookies? I tally the months in my head. Is he serious or just being friendly?

The truck comes to a stop, saving me from my thoughts. "We're here." He puts the truck in park.

"What's this?" I'm in awe of the massive cabin in front of me.

"It's my cabin." He looks over at me and for the first time I can see the insecurity, the need of approval...from *me*.

"It's huge."

"That's what she said." He winks, breaking the ice a little more.

"Always a comedian." I reach for the handle, but Kyle breaks our connection by reaching across my lap, stopping me. "Nina, chivalry's not dead."

"What?"

"Please, let me." He nods towards the door.

"Oh! Okay."

Tucking my hands in between my legs, I straighten my shoulders and sit a little taller, waiting for him to run around. I haven't really noticed it before, but it's always been there. Java Talk, Woody's, offering to take me home, helping me paint, letting me go first... always the gentleman.

I've been so set on proving myself I really haven't taken a look at the big picture. Kyle is almost too good to be true.

A good guy.

Hitting his hand on the hood, he hurries around to open my door. "After you m'lady." He waves his hand in a circular motion as he bows.

"Why thank you kind sir." I hold out my hand for him to take and step down doing a little curtsy.

Standing side by side, Kyle's hands now in his pockets, we stand there admiring his new cabin together.

"Did you just buy it?" I glance up at him.

Looking back down at me, unusually quiet. "I built it."

Eyes wide, I look between him and this monstrosity he calls a cabin. "This whole thing?"

This gets him to crack a smile. "The whole thing."

"You?"

"Me."

"Kyle, this is amazing. You built this with your own two hands?" I spin to stand in front of him.

"These..." He removes his hands from his pockets, holding them in front of him. "...some cool tools and big badass equipment, but yeah, I did."

Not even thinking, I grab both of his hands and hold them in mine. "These are amazing. You built that..." I let go of one hand to gesture over my shoulder. "A home. Your home."

A home I wish I had. Everything from the rockers on the wraparound porch to the tire swing off to the side screams family. It's everything I have ever dreamed about.

"You really know how to build one's ego." His gaze is fixed on mine as he begins to joke. "I should show you all the projects I have worked on."

"I would love that, but right now..." I begin walking backward, his hand still in mine. "I want to see what those hands built."

Not letting go, we walk hand in hand toward his home. Giving my hand a little squeeze, he whispers, "Thank you."

"For what?" I nudge his shoulder.

"For trusting in me."

Trust.

There's that word again. I did. I let go of my fears and had faith in a man I didn't really know. And now, instead of following, I'm leading myself to the unknown.

Chapter 16

KYLE

"Kyle, this...it's incredible." Nina, walks around the great room, twirling. "The ceilings are so tall and this..." She walks over to the picture window that showcases the woods surrounding the cabin.

"I have a confession." I walk up behind her, hands in pockets. The desire to touch her is almost uncontainable.

"Hmm?" She wraps her arms around herself as she turns to face me.

"I didn't exactly build this whole place by myself."

"Oh?" Her eyebrows scrunch together, doubt creeping up on her beautiful face.

"My dad." I hurry to get the words out before she has time to get in her own head. "This was his dream for me and my mom."

"It's a good dream." Her smile is weak. She holds out her hand, requesting mine. "Wanna hand hug?"

Nodding, I take her hand in mine. "Hand hugging while talking is always good."

I step next to her and we both become mesmerized by the darkness that is overcoming the summer sky.

"My dad, he owned Woody's. He was Woody."

Turning her head slightly, she looks up at me. "Do you look like him?"

"Yeah. Just a younger version," I answer. I'm not sure if she knows that she is setting me at ease, giving me time to tell the story I want to tell, but she is.

"Lewis men, very handsome."

"My mom thinks so." I rub circles around her thumb with mine. "She loved him so much. They had everything." I shake my head. "The memories are overwhelming at times. You would think after seventeen years it would get easier, but it doesn't."

"I understand." She takes my hand in both of hers. "So, tell me about this place."

"Well, my dad inherited this land from my grandfather, his dad. It had this small, run-down cabin that had no running water and a porch that barely could handle one rocking chair, let alone two."

"Two?"

"Yeah, it's kind of a neat story." My lips curl up at the memory. "He would come out here to get away from the world and when I was old enough, he let me tag along. One day he asked me what I thought about living here."

"I could only imagine what a young you thought of it." She giggles.

"Yeah, I wasn't too thrilled. Remember, no running water." I join in the laughter. "But I took him around the yard and told him what I thought it would take for us to be a family here."

"I bet he loved that." She pulls my arm a little closer. My arm is tangled in hers, hands hugging, shoulder to shoulder.

"He did. Each weekend he would bring me out here and

Love Conquer

together we would sit in these metal folding chairs at a card table, drawing out plans for our dream home."

"Patient man."

"Very much so. He taught me so much during that time. By twelve I knew how to draw out floor plans."

"Good to know." She beams.

"A few months before the accident, my dad and I built two rocking chairs and set them on that rundown porch. He set a milk crate upside down to use as a table. Surprised my mom by setting out two glasses of Lipton iced tea and the rolled-up plans for the cabin."

"That's so romantic."

"It really was. My dad fell head over heels in love with my mom in grade school and fought like hell to keep her every day."

"What did she say? Did she like it?"

"He blindfolded her and had me walk her up to the porch where he was standing behind her rocking chair. Of course, she was apprehensive, but warmed up to it quickly once she saw the plans."

"It never happened?" She looks up, eyes watering, mirroring mine.

I shake my head. "He died the next year, from a forklift accident. That is why I'm so adamant about wearing safety equipment. If he would have had his on, this house would have been his."

"I'm so sorry."

"Me too."

Her stomach chooses this moment to growl.

"Oh, my." She unhooks our arms and covers her face, fingers splayed. "So embarrassing."

"What's embarrassing is me just now feeding you." I hold out my arm, letting her lead the way. "Let's feed you."

"Have you even cooked in this kitchen?" She runs a finger over the countertop, then walks over and opens the cabinets. "Holy hell!"

"Yeah, I went a little crazy."

"A little?" She begins to open every cabinet and just watching her in here, feeling comfortable, gets me thinking things I shouldn't after less than a week. "You bought the whole store."

"I bought them after I put the finishing touches in the kitchen."

"Amish cabinets," she mumbles. "sTm." She brushes the cabinet with her hand, appreciating the design. "Why didn't you build them?"

"Honestly, you can't beat the craftsmanship that they put into it. Could I have done this? Yeah, but I wanted to be in this place within a year and it's been just about that since I started the place."

"You did all this in a year?" she asks in astonishment.

"Yeah."

"WilliamSon Construction during the day, you own Woody's..." She puts her finger to her chin. "Kyle, you had to work on this every night and weekend."

"Just about," I confess. "It kept me out of trouble."

I quickly turn before she can read anymore into that comment. This night is going better than I could have thought and I refuse to let any more of my past invade the night.

"How about shrimp alfredo?"

"I love it."

Love Conquer

"Good, it should only take twenty minutes or so start to finish." I reach into the cabinets, pulling out pots and seasoning.

"What can I do?" She looks around, unsure of what to do or where to sit.

I have two pieces of furniture, a bed and couch. Haven't made it to full livable status.

"Here." I set the pot down, going to stand in front of her. "Can I?"

"Yes."

Hands on her waist, I set her on the counter, her legs spread, welcoming. My hands slide to her hips, and I can't think. I take a step, inching myself closer. "Nina?" I'm so close. Her scent consumes me.

"Kyle."

"I need a hug." I opt for the cowardly way out.

"This would make five. You only get three more. So, choose wisely." She reaches around my neck and pulls me close to her.

Leaning back a little, I arch a brow. "This makes four."

Shaking her head, she pulls me back in, forcing herself to the edge of the counter. "Nope, window hand hug."

"I thought maybe that was a freebie." I lean in, rubbing my hands along her back. "You know, tragic story and all."

"Kyle Lewis." She leans back, smacking my chest. "Don't use that to get your way."

"Hey! No breaking the hug till I'm ready. You already cheated me out of one."

Her stomach growls again, a warning the hug has to end. Turning my face into her neck, I inhale her scent.

"Did you just sniff me?"

I tense, realizing I just got caught getting wrapped up in the moment. "Maybe." I take a step back. "Creepy?"

"Nah, I'm a sniffer too."

"Did you sniff me?" I reach into the freezer, grabbing the shrimp.

"I'm a professional, you wouldn't know if I did." She hops down off the counter and comes to my side. "I can't believe you know how to cook."

"Only child until my mom remarried. I guess you could say I was bored and liked the constant attention." I turn on the stove top, adding butter to the skillet. "You cook?"

"Just the basics, but nothing like this."

"This is pretty simple." I hand her the wooden spatula. "Here." I turn her toward the stovetop.

"Ummm?"

I stand behind her, reaching around to pour in the shrimp. "Push them around in the butter." I cover her hand with mine, forcing my other hand to go to the counter and not to her waist. "Yes, just like that."

"Mmm." She turns her face up toward mine. "Smells good." Her lips are so close, but as inviting as they are, I can't.

Self-control, Lewis. Think about port-a-potties. Those stink. Everything Nina is not.

"I'll grab the spices." I break away before she starts to notice exactly how turned on she makes me.

Port-a-potty.

"So, tell me about your family." I'm now back at her side, throwing in a dash of this and dash of that. "You found out a little about my parents and how I became who I am today. What about you?"

Tensing back up, she hands me the wooden spoon. "Can

you finish?"

"Nina, I didn't mean to..."

"I just need a minute. Do you care if I use the restroom?" She walks around the counter and heads toward the master bath I showed her during the tour.

I've obviously hit a nerve. I can only hope that since I was so open, she will feel comfortable enough to confide in me.

And if not, we still have hugs.

NINA

IT'S BEEN FOREVER SINCE SOMEONE even cared about my life, let alone what happened to my parents. Niki buried it deep within, refusing to talk to anyone.

I wanted to talk and I tried to with Brandon, but he told me the best medicine was moving on. Now, Kyle, he wants to know and after sharing his past, why not let him in on mine? Show him he isn't alone.

Excusing myself wasn't a cop-out. I wasn't running away from Kyle, not this time. I just needed a moment to deal with emotions I wasn't allowed to feel for so long.

Placing my hands on the sink, I lean forward and examine the new me. The person who is looking back is different. I'm not who I was when I was with Brandon, but I'm not the me from before him either. I'm changing.

Healing.

"Nina." Kyle is on the other side of the door. Just a day ago

I would have been embarrassed, but now, after he has opened himself up, showing me something so special and private, I know telling him will only help heal me.

"I'm coming." I swing open the door to see him leaning against the wall.

"I thought maybe you needed a hug." He opens his arms wide, inviting.

"How did you know?" I walk right into them and secretly breathe him in as his strong arms enclose me, securing me and my heart.

"A hugger just knows." I can feel his smile against my hair. "I caught that."

"Caught what?"

"You sniffed me." He brings his arms up, hands combing through my hair.

"Yeah, well, it comforts me." I push off the wall. Breaking free, another hug checked off the list. "Plus, you're hot," I holler back as I walk toward the kitchen. I'm shocked to find that plates and drinks are made. "Umm..." I point to the kitchen. "How long was I gone?"

"It doesn't take long." He walks over to the island, picking up the plates. "Can you get the drinks?"

"Sure." I grab the tea and follow him into the great room.

"This is the only table I have, for now." He sets the plates down and sits on the floor, patting a spot next to him.

"Best table ever." I crack a smile and cop a squat. "God, Kyle, this really does smell delicious." I begin to twirl a small bite around the fork, stabbing a shrimp to secure my noodles.

"I ran out of parmesan." He waits for me to take the first bite.

"Oh, my." I cover my mouth trying to talk and swallow. "It's soooo good." I roll my eyes to the back of my head.

"Good." He takes my response as his cue to dig in.

Setting my fork down, I decide now is the time.

"You asked about my family..."

"Nina..." He tries to swallow, grabbing for his tea to wash down the food. "You don't have to feel pressured. That's not what I wanted."

"I know." I reach out and grab his hand. I'm not sure if this time it's to comfort him or me. "I want to."

I pause, then begin my story. "Niki and I grew up in a family that had its ups and downs, but not because my parents didn't love each other. They really, really did." I reach for my cup. I'm not really thirsty, but need the break. "My parents were very much like yours except they were high school sweethearts, marrying as soon as they turned eighteen. Everyone thought my mom was pregnant, but they just didn't want to spend another night apart so they got married to avoid living in sin."

"Sounds like my parents," he says between bites.

"Since they got married so young they went straight to work building a life for a family they so desperately wanted. Skipping an education."

I roll the fork, going for a bigger bite this time.

"Sounds like they knew what they wanted. My mom did the same thing, but my dad, he took night classes to get his business degree." He waits for me to take another bite before he continues. "His father owned the lumber yard, which consisted of a small pole barn and metal fence. My dad built it to what it is today."

"My father always wished he would have done that, but once

they had Niki, he took on another job. Always gone." I take one more quick bite. "That's really good, but if I eat another bite, I'm going to explode." I push the plate away.

"Keep talking. I'm going to take these to the kitchen and clean up." Kyle stands, clearing away the plates. I follow, taking a seat on the couch that is only a couple feet away.

"With my father working so much, it created a divide within the family and arguments were part of the nightly routine. The weird thing about it though, it was fighting over wanting more time. That's all she wanted. Him."

"Did your mom still work when she had you guys?" He begins drying the dishes he washed while listening to me.

"Only for a minute, but she hated leaving Niki with strangers. So, she made up for it by watching other kids. That only lasted a little while. She didn't have the patience to deal with Niki and others. Niki was hard enough." I laugh thinking of some of the stories Mom used to tell.

"I can see that. She is something else."

"She really is a good person. Niki has just had a wall up for so long. Anyways, my life was just average, with parents who fought about needing to spend more time together."

"And now?" He comes strolling in, plopping down, arm across the back, facing me.

"Well, eventually things got better. He worked his way up in the factory to management. The house eventually was paid off. Niki and I were older so they were able to do more just the two of them."

"Did that upset you?" He lays a hand on my leg. Palm up. *Hand hug.*

Reaching out, I grab it, scooting a few inches closer. "Yes

and no. I mean, I loved that our parents were finally happy. When they were happy, Niki and I were too. You know?"

"Yeah."

"I'm just thankful they got to travel before my mom got sick..." I take a deep breath before saying the words I haven't said in years. "...with breast cancer." I look up to the ceiling, rubbing my temple with one hand, while still holding his with my other hand.

Kyle doesn't try to say anything. Just being here, listening, is enough.

"When she found the lump, it was too late. She tried to fight, but it took her over so fast..." The tears begin to fall and instead of running to the bathroom, I do the one thing I have been afraid to do, ask for help. "I need you."

I break my hands free to wipe the tears and before I can say anything else, Kyle is enveloping me in his arms. "I got you."

"Kyle, it was so bad. I was a senior in high school when my mom passed and my dad..."

"Shhhh..."

"He shut down, Kyle. He checked out and died of a broken heart. He fell asleep one night and didn't wake up the next day. Died of a massive heart attack."

In this moment, I release the years of holding it in, letting Kyle hold me as sobs rack my body.

"I got you," He whispers over and over again, rocking me in his arms. "It's going to be okay."

And here, right now, I know they will be because *he* makes me believe they will.

Chapter 17

NINA

"Hey sleepyhead," Kyle whispers in my ear.

"Mmm." I reach down and pull the blanket back up over the both of us.

Both.

Of.

Us.

Me.

Kyle.

Oh! My! God!

Throwing the cover back, I lift myself up, arching my back. "Did we?

"No, we didn't…I wouldn't." He reaches for me. "Come back."

"I need to go." I start to move to get up, but what he said has me wondering. "What do you mean you wouldn't?"

I really don't know why I even care. I'm not ready to get physical, but him stating it makes me wonder, *is it me?*

"Oh! I definitely would and if you keep on moving like that," he holds my hips down, trying to still my movements, "you are going to see exactly how much I want to." He winks.

"But, something tells me you aren't ready for that and Nina, I'm perfectly fine with it."

"Why do you have to go and say stuff like that?" I collapse back onto his chest, burying my face.

Last night, he held me until the tears stopped flowing and even then, he curled me under his arm while we watched movie after movie. I knew I should've had him take me home the minute we both started getting drowsy, but I didn't want the feeling to end. Especially after I got a taste of what this could be.

"Nina, don't go," he whispers a plea, brushing a simple kiss across my lips.

There was nothing sexual about it. Just a guy who wanted a girl to stay and a girl saying yes.

Staying the night wasn't really the plan. So, when I woke up after one of the best nights of sleep I ever had, I was confused until I felt him. A tad rough, yet tender.

"Well, I like to think honesty is the best policy." He chuckles, his laugh vibrating through me.

"Is that so?" I lift my head, covering my mouth to shield him from the dreaded morning breath.

"Yep." He pulls my hand down. "Don't hide."

"I haven't brushed." I put my hand back in place and he smiles.

"You're too damn cute." He grins, gum between his teeth.

"You have gum?" I bring my hands up, placing them on his chest.

"Sure do."

"Gimme."

"It's in my front pocket, just reach in..." He suddenly stops.

"What?"

"You better not." He places a hand on my lower back, shifting our bodies, to free a hand and secure me a piece of minty freshness.

"Oh!" I pretend to see what he's talking about, but it's the bulge further south that is causing me to get a little excited.

"Here." He unwraps the piece, placing it into my mouth and setting the wrapper on the coffee table.

"Honesty, right?"

"Always."

I chomp my gum really fast, getting the juices overflowing in my mouth, washing away the morning breath. "Can I get a hug?" I continue to chew.

"Of course. Remember, new day. This is one," he says as he sits us up, my body now wrapped around his. Parts of me covered, yet exposed.

"Now, will you kiss me?" I push the gum to the back of my mouth, waiting for him to follow through with my request.

"You want me to kiss you?" He continues the hug, contemplating.

"I mean, I do, but if you don't want to, I don't want to force you." I begin to let my imagination run wild. Did I misread this?

"Don't," he interrupts. He slams his mouth against mine, urgently at first, then soft, like I know him to be. Slow and seductive.

My body heats, as his hardens beneath me. Wrapping my arms under his, I snake them up his back, holding his head to me. My body responds and I begin to rock back and forth, the friction too much to handle.

"Nina," he breathes. "This—"

"More." I can't help it. It's been so long and this, what we are doing, isn't out of guilt. I'm not forced or expected. I want to do it.

He fights it at first; hands on my hips, he gently pushes me away.

I run my hands through his hair. I feel Kyle everywhere but where I want him the most. I know what I'm doing could lead to something else, and I'm not sure if I'm ready for it, but right now I'm selfish. I need this.

"Please." I pull back, sucking his lip into mine, before we lock gazes. "I want this. Anything more?" I shake my head. "But this, I need it. Please."

Without giving it a second thought, his lips are back on mine. Hands on hips, he pulls me forward causing me to gasp. Tongues lashing, teeth grazing. I have never felt something like this. With him, it feels so good.

Lifting his hips he finds where I want him. Rotating, rubbing. I can feel him getting harder and it turns me on to know that I'm doing this to him. *Me.*

The way his body is reacting to mine has me on edge. Leaning forward, knees on the couch, I grind down, finding my sweetest spot.

"Kyle..." I breathe his name.

Back, forth.

"I-I feel so good."

Harder, faster.

"I'm...oh God." I throw my head back and twist and rotate my hips with each pulsating release inside of me.

"Nina..." He brings me back down, kissing my neck. Licking, sucking.

Crap!

I was so caught up in the moment that I didn't think about the aftermath.

"I'm sorry." I slump forward, hanging my head in shame.

"Don't." Placing a finger under my chin, he lifts my head so we're eye to eye. "That was one of the most beautiful things I have ever experienced. Don't discredit it by being embarrassed." He brushes his lips against mine.

"What about you?" I worry my bottom lip.

"Shower, cold one."

"I could..." I try to come up with something. Maybe an offer, I'm unsure.

"No." He picks me up and sets me beside him, the bulge painfully obvious through his shorts. "This was about you. I gave you what you needed and in return it was equally as satisfying for me."

"There is no way," I raise an eyebrow, pointing to the obvious, "that satisfied you."

"You have no idea." He leans over, kissing me on the nose. "Breakfast?"

"I'm starving."

He just doesn't realize how hungry I am.

Him.

This moment.

It released something in me that I didn't know was there. A need to be fed something more. What exactly? I'm not sure, but it's *more* than I was capable of before.

Love Conquer
KYLE

Out of everything I could have fixed her, she chooses cereal.

"Are you sure you don't want some protein to go with that?" I feel a little bad for fixing myself eggs and bacon while she downs the leftover milk from a bowl of Cookie Crisp.

"Well, maybe some bacon." She sets the bowl down and begins to scan the room. "Did you hear that?"

"Hear what?"

"Shhh!" She holds her hand out. "That beep, do you hear it?"

"I think your..." I hear a series of chimes. "Yep! That's a phone going off."

"What time is it?" she asks frantically.

"Don't worry, it's only nine and it's Sunday. You're off." I turn off the burner and remove the eggs.

"Niki!" She takes off for the couch, skidding to a stop. "I forgot to tell her I wasn't coming home."

"Oh shit!" I'm right beside her looking under cushions.

"Here!" She holds up her phone. "It was under the blanket."

Unlocking her phone she begins to scan the texts. Her face drains of color.

"Ummmm...Kyle..." She turns to face me. "I think it was your phone."

"What? Why?"

My phone is pinging with text after text. Turning in circles, I try to see where it's coming from.

"Under the couch, try there." She looks at her phone again. "This isn't good."

Bending down, I look back at her. "It's going to be fine. You are twenty-three." I reach under the sofa, finding my phone. "What could she possibly do?" I swipe it alive. "Holy shit!"

"Right?" she confirms. "What did she say?"

Niki: You're DEAD!

Followed with a Scarface GIF *Say hello to my little friend.*

Niki: BYE-BYE BALLS!
Niki: First the right.
Niki: Then the left.
Niki: No hope of having kids.
Niki: You could adopt, but hello DEAD!

Followed with a middle finger GIF. Then a voice clip. Nina's eyes are about to pop out of her head. "Is that..."

Niki: Guess what tool I'm using.
Niki: Oh? Too busy fucking my sister, eh?
Niki: It's a grinder. Just in case you were wondering.

She sends another GIF of a machete.

Niki: To sharpen this knife.
Niki: To cut off your twig and berries!

"What's she sayin'?" Nina is over my shoulder. "Oh. My. God."

"Nina, it's your sister, she's worried about you." I reach over, pulling her under my arm. "She doesn't mean it."

Holding her phone in front of me, she shows me one text.

Niki: Kyle is D.E.A.D.

"Just call her and let her know you are okay."
"Kyle?"
"Yeah?"
"I need a hug."
"You got it." I pull her in tight. "She's just looking out for you, but to be on the safe side, we better not let this happen again. Cause my balls, I kinda like them."
"How about I just leave a voice message?" She nods her head eagerly.
"I'll clean up. You confess to our sins." I smile.
She blushes.
"Maybe not all of them." She twists out of my arms and heads to the door. "I better take this outside."
"Tell her I'll have you home within the hour." I shout after her.
Before tucking my phone back in to my shorts, I scan the messages again. "Damn, Niki." I reach down, grabbing my balls and whispering, "I promise, I won't let anything happen to you."

The ride home is a little quiet. Even though Nina said everything was okay I can tell something is worrying her.
"Are you okay?" I reach over, giving her knee a little squeeze.
"Yeah." She pats my hand slowly, obviously not sure if she wants it there or not.
"What's going on?" I lay my hand, palm up on the center

console.

"What exactly happened with Cindy?" She keeps looking forward, but reaches over and grabs onto my hand.

Giving her a little squeeze, I let her know it's going to be okay.

"I was married," I confess. There is no other way around this than to come clean.

"To Cindy?" She turns to face me, our hands still connected.

"Oh no! But I drowned out the past by spending time with her."

Saying the words out loud make me feel like the biggest dick. Even though we agreed on our arrangement, she made it into something it wasn't.

"You used her for sex?" She tilts her head, waiting for my confession.

"At first, yes, but then just to feel normal again. I took her on a few dates. We watched movies—"

"Did you cook for her?" she interrupts.

We're a block away from Niki's so I pull over and twist to face her.

"I don't know what your sister told you, but last night..." I close my eyes, remembering everything. "It was a first for me." I open them back up to see Nina watching my mouth, waiting for the words that could devastate her. I refuse to be that man, the one who breaks her heart. I want to be the one who heals it. Reaching over, I caress her cheek with my free hand, and she leans into my touch. "Being with you is different, and not in the way you think either."

"Then how? You've known me less than a week, how do you know?"

Love Conquer

"I'm not sure what is going to come of this, but what I do know is I want to spend as much time with you as possible."

"I do too." Her voice is barely a whisper.

"Then don't doubt this."

"Kyle, it's not you I doubt, it's me." She turns her head, gazing out the window.

"Well, then we are in luck." I give her hand a little squeeze. "Because I believe in you."

"Kyle..." She swings her head around, tears forming.

"Let's get you home." I throw it into drive and ease it back onto the road. "Before your sister has my balls."

That gets her to giggle. "Yeah, she's waiting."

After a few moments, we pull up to an irate Niki, wearing a white apron and a welding mask and sharpening a butcher knife.

"Ummm. I'm going to go."

"Don't worry, she's all bark and no bite." She leans over, giving me the gentlest of kisses before she sits back in her seat.

"Thank you," I whisper.

Still scared of losing my balls, I mentally count the seconds it would take to run around the truck and open the door.

You can do it.

I give myself a pep talk, fling open the door, leaving it ajar for an easy getaway, and run around, letting Nina out.

"She's looking at us." She takes hold of my hand and jumps down.

"Don't look." I turn her around.

"Thank you for the wonderful date. It was nice." Nina wraps her arms around my middle for the biggest of bear hugs from such a petite person.

Looking over her shoulder I see Niki, standing there, watching, helmet up over her head. A look of understanding crosses her face as she turns and walks away.

Chapter 18

NINA

"Niki! If you want to do this, let's do this."

I come barreling through the door, ready to take whatever she has to give me.

"I was wrong." She peeks her head up over the couch.

"Wh-what?"

"That?" She points from me to outside. "He adores you." She comes over and stands directly in front of me. "The way he touched you, the look...I was wrong."

I begin to shake with laughter. "You were basically dangling his balls in front of him for keeping me overnight and now?"

"Nina, don't be a dick. I said I was wrong." She eyes me as she passes to the kitchen. Opening her cabinet, she runs her finger along the mugs until she finds the one she wants: *#coffeesaveslives*. Holding it up, she points to it then dares me to say something.

"Oh, is that a silent threat?" I throw my head back defiantly.

"Is that what you think it is? It's just a mug, Nina." She fills it, leaving a little coffee in the pot. "Kids, don't try this at home." She holds the pot to her lips and downs the rest. Not quite a full cup, but more than a sip.

"You're something else." I pull out a barstool, taking a seat at the island to watch her occupy herself with everything but me.

"Come on, Nik, talk to me."

"What's there to say that hasn't already been said?" She stands across from me.

"Niki!" I slap the table, startling myself. "You went bat-shit crazy this morning. I need to know where that was coming from."

"Fine." She begins to pace. "I have been racking my brain with how I let you down." She stops, staring at me. "Because I have. The past few years, I have been so wrapped up in my own life that I didn't notice I knew nothing about yours. If I would have—"

"No!"

"If I would have asked more questions, demanded to see you..." She comes to stand beside me. "Nina, last summer, when you broke your foot. Did he hurt you?"

Clasping my hands over my head, I fight off the demons, the ones knocking on the door to memory lane.

"I can't go there." I drop my hands to my side and now I'm the one wearing out the floor. I can't let myself remember.

"I knew it. He fucking put his hands on you."

"Not exactly. It's not as simple as it seems." I try to give her peace of mind.

"Nina, if I would have visited, I could have stopped it." She places a hand on my back and in this moment, I don't want my sister. I don't want her comfort and especially not her pity.

"I didn't even know. Don't you get it? If I couldn't stop it, what makes you think you could have?" I jerk away. "I loved that man. For every single bad quality he had something good. I wanted to believe he could change." I throw myself down in the chair, looking over at her. I sigh. "How could you save me from something I didn't know I needed saving from?" I'm up again, not sure what to do or where to go. "I had to find the strength within. Only I could say when enough was enough."

"I promised Mom I would watch after you." A tear streaks down her cheek. "I failed."

"Niki, you didn't. Don't you see?" I spin her around. "Look at where we are. You have a wonderful relationship, engaged to your best friend and I'm here, safe, with you."

"Gavin *is* pretty damn awesome." Her smile is bright, one reserved for only him.

"Yes, he is." I hold out my arms for her. "Hug me."

"Hmm."

"Just trust me." I wave her in.

"This is kinda nice." She taps on my back.

One.

Two.

Three.

Four.

"How long do we hold on?" she continues to count.

Five.

"Is there a pop-up timer or something?"

Six.

Seven.

"You totally take the fun out of hugging." I break free.

"Nina, I'm sorry about this morning. I just wanted to protect you. I thought—"

"I know and I thank you, but in all reality, I should have

messaged you. Adult or not, I'm staying at your house. I shouldn't have made you worry."

"Yeah! That's what I meant!" She flips me the bird, smirking. "Screw you for making me worry." She heads down the hall hollering back, "Love you!"

"You have to!" I shout back.

Reaching into my pocket, I pull out my phone to let Kyle know everything is okay.

Me: Everything is fine. You get to keep your balls.

He must have been waiting because as soon as I fire off the text, the bubbles are there teasing me with a message being typed.

Kyle: Thank goodness. I was just saying my goodbyes.

"Hey Nina, I have a surprise for you." Niki comes in the room dangling a key in front of me.

Holding my finger up, I press the microphone to send a voice text.

Me: Got to go. Call you later.

"What's this?" I pull the key off her finger.

"It's the key to your new house." She bounces with excitement.

"What do you mean, *my new house*?"

"Well, it just so happens that the renter moved out of my old place."

"Wait, you mean..." I try to contain myself, just in case it's not what I think it is.

"Gavin and I talked about it and thought you should move

in. Have your own place."

"Oh! My! God!" I begin to jump up and down, screaming. Niki joins in.

We are so wrapped up in dancing and jumping around that we don't see Gavin come in. Reaching for Niki's hand he starts jumping with us, squealing like a schoolgirl.

"What are we screaming for?" Gavin shouts.

Stopping suddenly, I look over at Niki. "Is he always like this?"

"Yeah." She shrugs her shoulders. "He's a girl."

"Take that back." He lifts Niki up, throwing her over his shoulder. "Me Tarzan, you Jane."

"Oh Lord!" She pounds his back. "Put me down, I get it. You are man hear you roar. Yada, yada, yada."

"Tarzan take woman to bed." Gavin turns to wink at me. "Congratulations."

"Thank you! You guys rock." I turn and swing my new key from my index finger.

What would one do with their new-found freedom? SHOUT IT FROM THE ROOF — or living room in this instance. So, I dig out my phone to call Kyle, hoping he can celebrate with me.

"Miss?"

I spin to see a man in uniform at the front door, which Gavin apparently left open.

"Yes?"

"Are you Miss Niki Sanders?"

"What's going on out here?" Gavin comes from around the corner, Niki right behind him.

"You left the door open. This guy is asking for Niki." I look at her. "What did you do?"

"Niiiiiiki?"

"For Pete's sake, Gavin. I paid the damn parking tickets." She rolls her eyes. "You miss one ticket and all hell breaks loose."

"No tickets. I just need to give her this." The man waves a manila envelope around.

Gavin holds out his hand to take it.

"Actually, I need to give this to Miss Sanders."

"Good Lord, you would think I was being served or something." Niki pushes past us, grabbing the envelope.

"Miss Sanders, consider yourself served." The deputy walks off.

"You got to be..." She rips open the envelope, scanning the contents. "Shit motherfucker." She throws it on the coffee table.

"What's going on?" I ask, but am ignored.

"Gav? What am I going to do?" She sits on the couch, face buried in her hands.

Picking up the papers, he scans through them. "Well, looks like they just need you to testify in the custody case of Tucker Alexander."

"I'm not sure...Wait, what? She gave him Aiden's last name?"

"Since you were his teacher and involved with all parties they are calling on you as a character witness." Gavin sits down beside his fiancée.

"Gav..."

"I know babe..."

"Guys?" I plop down in the chair across from them.

"Aiden is the one who was in the middle of that situation that went down last summer."

"Ohhh! That's the guy?" I glance at Niki from the corner

of my eye.

"Yep, that's the asshole." Gavin throws the papers down before he climbs back on the couch, pulling her with him. "We will figure this out."

"Niki, I'm here to stay. I'll go with you. Whatever you need. I'm here."

Lifting her head, she gives me a weak smile. "Thanks, Nina."

Deciding I'm just interfering, I slip away to my room for a little nap. After everything last night and now today, I can't help but let the exhaustion take over.

Tomorrow is a new day.

Chapter 19

NINA

It's been a couple weeks since I got the keys to the house and thankfully, Niki gave me the time to get it cleaned up before I moved in. Plus, I needed to save money. Even though I'm staying rent free for the summer, I still need things. Furniture for one.

Deciding to take a break I head up to the coffee shop to see Jen, but as I walk in, something catches my eye.

The couple.

Walking out of the same door that I'm going in is the couple from a few weeks ago, but today instead of looking afraid and uneasy, she's smiling and laughing.

Was I going crazy?

"Hi." I wave, trying to catch her eye, but they both act as if I'm not even there.

Did he threaten her?

Did I imagine it?

Hurrying inside, I run to Jen, who I know is working a double. "Who was that couple?"

"The one that just left?" she replies.

"Yeah, are they regulars?" I ask, hoping she has something

that could put me at ease.

"Not really. I mean I've seen them, but not like the others." She grabs a cup and starts making an order. "Why? What's going on?"

"Just something I've noticed, but I'm not sure if I'm being crazy or not."

She pushes the drink toward me. "Six eighty-five."

"What?"

"I'm going on break. You're buying us drinks." She holds out her hand.

"You're a mess." I dig in my purse, pulling out a ten.

"That is neither here nor there." She rings me up, handing back the change. "Corner booth. Gossip session."

"Got it."

Balancing the coffees, I head toward the corner, taking a seat, waiting for Jen so I can get her input on a few things for the house.

It's kind of crazy if you think about it. Just a few weeks ago, it took everything I had to step through those doors, but today, I live for the unknown. I *crave* it. Each day is a new adventure on the quest to finding myself, to finding where I belong.

KYLE

"I HAVE TO TELL YOU, Lee, I think you're alright." I give him a firm clasp on the back.

"I bet you do." He shuts the tailgate. "You couldn't have got all that," he points his thumb over his shoulder, "without me."

"Fine. You have me there." I reach into the cooler and get him a water.

"I helped you do all that and this is what I get?" he jokes, taking the bottle from my hand and chugging it down.

"Help me take it over to Nina's and I'll buy you dinner and a round of drinks." I throw the cooler over the side and round the truck.

Heading towards the passenger side, Lee opens the door, and stalls. "Dinner, drinks and you stop giving me hell at work." He dares me to refuse.

"Deal." I wave my hand. "Now get in."

Climbing in, he buckles up. "Does Nina know you did all this?"

"Not exactly. She's expecting me though."

"Don't you think it would have been helpful to tell her?" He starts fiddling with the radio.

"Don't touch that." I smack his hand away. "It's called a surprise for a reason. Plus, this stuff is just to get her started."

"That's cool." He scans the area. "This is a nice neighborhood."

"It's a quaint little subdivision"

I turn onto her road and see her unloading some things from Niki's car, looking damn hot in cut-off jean shorts and a barely-there tank.

"And here she is." I pull into her drive.

"Holy shit! She's even hotter out of uniform." Lee's leaning forward checking out what I have seen so many times in the past week.

Throwing my arm out. I push him back. "That..." I nod over

to Nina who is totally oblivious to how sexy she really is. The little sway in her walk, in those short shorts, is a huge turn on. "Is not for your viewing pleasure."

My eyes only.

"So you're the alpha male type?"

"What? No! I mean, I don't think so." I'm trying to figure out what he meant. "Nina takes care of herself."

"Chill, Lewis. I was just giving you a hard time." He holds out his fist for me to bump.

"Just help me get this unloaded." I hop out, catching Nina as she's coming back out.

"Kyle! What's all this?" She walks up, hand shielding her eyes.

"Well, this is a table for the kitchen and that's a couch for your living room and behind that over there is a box of supplies that I thought you could use."

I stand waiting for her approval, nervous that maybe Lee was right. Is this too big of a gesture? Did I take it too far?

"Please tell me you didn't pay for all that?" She steps around me and looks over the side of the truck bed.

"Nope, it's all borrowed or donated." I stand beside her, wrapping my arm around her waist to bring her in. "Drew had an extra table and couch when he moved in with Aubrey and the supplies are random from me." I wink.

"You shouldn't have." She looks at me, blocking the sun. "Oh." She laughs, dropping her hand. "I should have had you here all day. Put you to work as my built-in sun blocker."

This girl. Sometimes she says the quirkiest things, but damn if it isn't as cute as hell.

"Let's get this unloaded so we can send this guy home." I

signal toward Lee.

"Standing right here." He raises his hand.

Nina gives me a sideward glance and walks over to him. "Lee, nice to meet you. I've seen you in Java Talk a few times and this guy only says great things about you."

"The *pleasure* is all mine." He takes her hand, a wicked smile plastered across his face.

Count that dinner goodbye, kid.

"Nina, you're going to build the kid's ego," I tell her over the truck.

"Kid? He's what?" She looks him over. "Twenty-three?"

"Yeah, but he's right. I got to get this unloaded before my ride comes to pick me up."

"At least let me fix you guys dinner." She begins to worry her bottom lip. "Well, by fixing, I mean picking up the phone to order a pizza."

"He has to leave," I bark, stressing to Lee that he better not mess with our plan.

"He's right. I really do." He looks at his watch. "We have twenty minutes to get everything unloaded."

"Then I guess we better get a move on it," she agrees.

"You just grab the door and tell us where you want it."

"Alrighty then," she says as she takes off for the house.

Pulling down the tailgate, Lee jumps up and starts to push the couch to the edge. "Kyle, man, you are one lucky son of a bitch."

"Don't I know it."

Love Conquer

"I can't believe you did all this." She comes out of the kitchen with two red plastic cups. "Tea?"

Taking one from her hand, I down it. "Lipton?"

"Of course. I went to the store beforehand and bought what I needed to make sure I had it on hand."

"I could have drunk water."

"And I could have sat on the floor," she says plopping down on the couch.

"Touché." I follow her down.

"Kyle..."

I can already tell she's letting something bother her. Not saying a word, I lay my hand out, palm up.

Watching my movements, she grins from ear to ear, taking my hand. "I don't have the money to pay for those supplies right now."

"You don't have to." I give her hand a little squeeze. Laying my head back, I roll it to the side to see her reaction.

"I wanted to do this on my own."

I shift to look at her. "Consider it a house warming gift."

"Gift?"

"Yeah. A gift."

"Gifts are good." She gives me a lazy smile. An accepting one.

"They are." I stand and walk over to an unopened box and cooler. "I also have this." I pull out the new air mattress and set of sheets. "And brought us some dinner." I slide the cooler over and open it.

"Ohhhh! Real food!"

"I made subs and a few sides. I thought with the temps being record high, this would-be kind of nice."

"It is." She pulls out a sandwich.

"Nope." I grab it and return it to the cooler.

"Hey!" Nina claws for me to give it back.

"Let's call it a night. The rest of the stuff we need to do can wait till tomorrow." I search for the bag that has a couple towels. "Here they are." I throw one at her. "Let's take a nice cool shower, get into clean clothes and veg out on this thing while we eat." I kick the mattress box over to her.

Her eyes are wide and I can see the wheels turning. "Separate showers."

"Oh?"

"It's better that way...well maybe not better, but necessary."

"Oh."

"Do you want to go first or me?"

"I guess me." She stands and heads toward the hallway.

Bending down, I pick up the mattress and begin to set it up.

"Kyle?" I look down the hall and see Nina, still fully dressed, with tears in her eyes. "Thank you for all this. For being you. Just...thank you."

"Always." I bring my fist up to my chest and rub the spot that now beats for her. The constant pounding reminds me that I will always do anything for her.

Chapter 20

NINA

Even though a cool shower sounds nice, my body is exhausted. I need the warm water to sooth my muscles that are worn after cleaning. This place was a mess, the guy who lived here after Niki was filthy!

Throwing on a pair of sleep shorts and a tank, I pad out to the front room. Kyle is just putting the finishing touches on our little picnic.

"I didn't think of bringing blankets, but I did buy you some new sheets." He fluffs out the top one, laying it over the mattress. "Just a little stiff."

"That's good," I giggle. "I'm not sure how big that hot water tank is, but I don't think I used it all up." I wink, tying my hair up and sitting down on the couch.

"I just need to rinse off." Kyle pushes himself off the floor. "I'll be..." He stands, his eyes raking over my body before they land on my chest. "Quick. I'll be quick."

Looking down, I notice I forgot a bra, and I'm apparently on high alert. "I-I...I can change." I stand, my face heating from his stare.

"No." He shakes his head as he walks over to me and bends

down. "You are so beautiful. Never hide." He lifts my chin, claiming my lips as his. Soft and tender and over way too soon. "I promise, quick."

"Mmm-hmm." I nod my head slowly, eyes still closed.

"Everything is ready. Just get comfortable over there." He grabs his towel out of the bag and a pair of shorts he brought in from his truck.

Leaning back on the couch, I take it all in. Today has been a breakthrough. No more comparisons. Kyle has shown me time and time again that he is nothing like Brandon.

Every move, every kind deed isn't just a choice. It's his nature, everything that he has learned from his family.

Family...

A thought crosses my mind as I stare across the room. A small box sits in the corner with a few cleaning supplies.

Tip-toeing down the hall, I hear the water still running. Not sure how much time I have, I run and grab the box and dump everything out, then put the box beside the bed. Standing back, I take it in.

Not right.

I bend down and try to lift the air mattress, but it's too awkward. Flopping it back down I get down on all fours and push it till it hits the front of the couch. Then I throw one box on one side and hurry to my bedroom where I know there is another one. I dump out its contents and put it on the other side of the mattress.

I study the scene again.

Almost.

Flipping open the cooler, I get out the sub and sides. Everything was to be split, but instead of bringing plates he brought plastic ware so we could share. Yanking the blanket, my makeshift curtain, down from the window, I toss it over the bed, laying the food on top.

Running to the kitchen I fill two cups up with tea and set one on each box. Spinning in circles, I look for what I need next, the final touch, and my eyes land on my bag in the corner. Hurrying over, I pull out a pen and the sketchbook I keep on me at all times. Yanking out a page, I write:

K.
You are always the brightest part of my day.
xoxo
N.

Quickly rolling it up, I reach for the band in my hair and secure the note. I place it by the tea on his box.

Perfect!

"What's this?" Kyle comes walking in before I can get into place.

I spin around. "Holy..." My jaw drops at the vision before me. Kyle looks great with clothes on, but Kyle without a shirt? I'm pretty sure I have drool leaking from the side of my mouth. It's summer for Pete's sake. Why haven't I seen him without a shirt before now?

"You like what you see?" He comes over to wrap his arms around me, but the closer he gets the further I back away. "Hey, come back here."

"You are...I don't even know what to say." I stop, letting him come to me. "Can I touch you?"

"Maybe later, but first..." He reaches out. "Hug time."

I nod. "That sounds like a plan."

As soon as our bodies connect, I know that I need more than the occasional kiss. I need him. All of him.

"Nina?" He speaks into my hair.

"What?"

"This?" He turns me around. My back to his front, he holds me close. "You remembered?"

"Well, I know this isn't your house and I don't have rocking chairs, obviously, but I wanted to show you that..." I trail off, opting to let the note say it all.

Walking around me, he sits down on the bed. He holds his hand out for me to follow and I do, climbing in beside him.

Reaching over, he takes a swig of his tea before he grabs the note, unrolls it and reads.

"Kyle, I just wanted—"

"Shhhh." He lays the note down and crashes his lips to mine.

He rolls me over, pushing the sandwich to the side and kisses me, wild and consuming. I never want these kisses to end. Moving between my legs and on top of me, his mouth lowers back to mine.

Nipping.

I feel his teeth scrape my bottom lip.

Licking.

His tongue traces the seam of my mouth.

I can't help the moan that escapes as my mouth falls open, inviting him in. Needing more. The way he hardens against me, I can tell he feels the same.

He pushes my tank up. Skin on skin. The only barrier now is his shorts and mine, and knowing this turns me on even more. I lift myself to meet his movement, loving the friction.

Love Conquer

My body pleads for a release, just from moving together in rhythm with our mouths. He whispers, "just this," against my lips. I shake my head and move my hands, rubbing his back as I lower them to his ass, wrap my legs around him and pull him down, my hips meeting his.

"I need you now. I just want to feel you."

Stopping, he looks me in the eyes, searching for approval, not wanting to take advantage of hormones going crazy. Knowing he's trying to hold back, to make sure I'm ready, only makes me want him more.

Working his way down, his eyes never leave mine. I raise my head to watch his descent. Collarbone, then lower. His mouth finds one nipple, taking it in and swirling his tongue over it, before switching to the other nipple. Back and forth. Sucking, pleasuring, in a way that is caring, pure adoration. My head falls back; the sensation is too much and my body arches up to his mouth. His hands drag down my sides, holding me in place, but his firm touch is gentle and I know I'm safe with him.

His lips move lower, lighting fires in their wake. Reaching my navel, swirling, dipping, his tongue dances on my skin.

I lean up once more and find his eyes on mine again, his smile teasing as he licks his way back up. My hips buck in reflex, wanting more. He presses a kiss to my chest, right in between my breasts, before his mouth heads south again, this time bringing my shorts down.

His hands on me, his mouth. Our bodies pressed together like he was made for me and I for him.

The wetness of his mouth, the air hitting damp skin causes me to shiver from a million sensations I've never experienced, never knew what I was missing. From that first swipe of his tongue up my center, I nearly see stars.

Pausing, he looks up once again, a handsome yet wicked smile on his face as his finger finds my core, hovering right there. Watching, waiting. Making sure. My heart melts as I nod in approval. One finger, sliding in and out, teasing me. Then two, and my eyes close as my hands find his hair, the pleasure all-consuming.

Using fingers, mouth, tongue, he's everywhere. His free hand finds my nipples once more while he devours me.

A few more licks, swipes and a twist of the hand. It doesn't take long before a tidal wave of pleasure crashes through me, and he laps it up greedily, the hum of his approval against my center. My body slowly comes down as he takes my legs in his hands, pulling me to him, and places gentle kisses on my thighs before he works his way up.

Once he settles between my legs, I open my eyes and find him staring at me. Both our breathing is heavy, no words are spoken.

He's still hard, and I want to return the favor. I want to show him the same pleasure he just showed me. I reach my hand toward the waist of his shorts, and he pulls back. I look at him confused.

He shakes his head. "It's not about me."

"But..." I reach for him again. "Please, Kyle. Just let me..."

He brings my hand to his lips and kisses it, before squeezing my palm against his and placing our joined hands above our heads. He leans in close and takes my lips once more in a whisper of a kiss.

"We have plenty of time. This was about you."

"I want you to feel pleasure, too."

"Nina, that gave me more than you can imagine."

He sits back on his heels and I sit up as well, bringing my knees to my chest, feeling exposed.

As if sensing my doubt, he pulls me to him. "We don't have to rush it. This was incredible. *You* were incredible."

I nod, unable to say any words, fearing my voice may tremble.

"But I may need another shower." He kisses me before climbing off the mattress. His confession makes me smile.

Lying back down, I pull the sheet over me. The tears that threaten to fall aren't because I feel rejected. Just the opposite, they're because I felt wanted. *Feel wanted*. And knowing what it's like to release my body to someone who wanted nothing but me. To bring me pleasure. It's a feeling I want more of.

Kyle is healing me. One touch at a time.

KYLE

"This sandwich is amazing." Nina tries to cover her mouth, but it's no use. She's pretty damn hungry.

"I can tell."

"I mean it's really good...." The sauce drips down her hand. "What kind of spread is this?" She runs her tongue along the edge and I can't help but groan.

"What?"

"If you keep eating the sandwich like that?" I grab her wrist and bring it to my lips to lick the sauce that drips down. "I won't be able to contain myself." I lick my lips.

"It's just...the best." She shovels it in, wadding up the wax paper to throw into our makeshift trashcan. "You know what? I could get used to this," she says, falling back on the bed.

Setting my sandwich down on my box, I brush the crumbs off the blanket and lay down, facing her.

"You look tired." I reach over, brushing a few strands of hair off her face.

"I am," she confesses. "Had a little bit of a workout, so to speak." She brings the sheet up over her mouth to hide her smile.

"Don't." I pull it back down, leaning in for a little kiss. "Everything about you is beautiful. Please don't hide it."

"I just feel like this is twice that I—"

"This is twice that I felt like I should give you something that you needed." I reach over to pull her in close.

"What about you?" She tucks her head in the crook of my neck. Her hand traces words on my chest. What? I'm not sure.

"When you are ready, I have no doubt that it will be something explosive." I bend down to kiss the top of her head. "You will be worth the wait."

"I hope I don't disappoint you." She looks up at me through her lashes. Not wanting to miss the moment, I lean back to gaze into those emerald jewels.

"There is no way. Right now? I could do this forever," I say as her fingers continue to write. "I'm trying to make out what you're spelling."

H.

O? No...A.

"I didn't even realize I was doing it, but yeah. I guess I am."

P.
P.
Y.

"Happy."

"Yeah. It's been forever since I felt that way and you...bring that out in me." She falls on her back with the biggest grin.

"Here let me." I lift up her tank, displaying a perfect canvas.

"No way, Kyle. There is no freakin' way I can handle all that again."

"No." I can't help but laugh at her reaction. "My turn to write something."

S.
P.
E.
C.
I.
A.
L.

"Can you spell it out again?" She closes her eyes, taking it all in.

"Any guesses?" I draw it out one more time, just to feel her skin under my fingertips.

"Oh sorry...I got lost in your magical touch. *Special*. It just felt too good to answer."

"My turn."

"Give me your hand," she says. "Palm up."

Doing as she requests, I wait for the word, but this time she draws a heart and closes it back up.

"You have mine."

I bring my hand to my chest. "Then I will cherish it."

We lie quietly for a few minutes until I break the silence.

"Meet my parents," I blurt out.

"Say what?" She has a frantic look on her face, making me think everything I thought we were working for may not be what it seems.

"You don't have to. I just have this birthday party I have to go to next weekend and I don't want to go alone."

"Oh! So, it's not like an official meet the parents kind of thing." She rolls over to face me now. Her eyebrows are scrunched up and she's worrying her bottom lip.

"If it is, would it be so bad?"

Please say no.

"Actually, No. I would love to," she says, but her face is still etched with worry.

"They are totally fine. Plus, my stepbrother and his family will be there. It's my niece's second birthday."

"It's not them. I mean it is, but...Kyle, I haven't ever 'met the parents' before." She scoots in closer. "What if they don't like me? What would that mean? Kyle, you can't date someone your parents hate."

"I happen to adore you and I know for a fact that my mom just wants me to be happy. To experience a fraction of what she has not just with my dad, but with her second husband."

"What should I wear? Can you help me figure out something to bring? Do you even bring something to a birthday party? What about a present? Do I help you or get my own gift? I don't know what to do."

I can't help it. She's so freaking adorable when she's nervous. I try not to laugh, but holding it in is just making my body tremble.

She smacks my chest. "It's not funny."

"They will love you."

"I hope so." She rolls me onto my back.

"Don't even think about it. I'm all showered out," I warn.

"No showers necessary." She winks as she sits up, pulls her tank over her head and lays back down. My dick instantly hardens.

"I think you underestimated yourself."

She lays half on me, an arm thrown over my chest, her leg intertwined with mine. "I just wanted to feel you."

"Shit. You saying stuff like that makes you even harder to resist."

"Will you please stay? Sleep with me, just like this?" she leans down, kissing my chest. Just one soft little peck.

"Always."

There is nowhere else I would rather be.

Chapter 21

NINA

I NEVER WANTED TO NEED someone. I thought I could do this all own my own, come here and start over. But sometimes even the strongest person needs someone to hold them up and Kyle, he lifts me up.

"Hey beautiful. You ready to go eat some carnival food and ride some rides until we get sick and come home?"

"Can we leave out the getting sick part?"

"Sure. Then we better skip that one spinning ride. It gets me every damn time." He walks around the room, picking things up before we leave.

"You don't have to do that." I reach in my purse, digging out whatever makeup I can find. "I can do that as soon as I'm done putting this on." I hold up my lip gloss and mascara.

"I made it. I clean it." He winks. "You can thank my momma on Sunday for raising me like a gentleman."

"Thank you." I head to the bathroom to apply a little color.

"Do you think we should take Niki's car back for the weekend?" I hear Kyle down the hall.

"Yeah. That's a great idea. I'll text her."

Me: I'm bringing your car back for the weekend.

Love Conquer

Niki: You don't need it?
Me: I'm with Kyle.
Niki: Did he stay the night?
Me: You going to be home?

I avoid the question. After the other day, I thought she was beginning to warm up to the idea, but maybe not.

Niki: What are you going to do for a car all weekend?

"Are you spending the night tonight?"
"Yep."

Me: Kyle's spending the night.

I wait for her reaction, but nothing. Not even the dots that show someone's typing. Just nothing.

Me: Niki, he really is a great guy.

Still nothing.

Me: We haven't had sex.
Niki: Don't. Not until you are ready. You got it?

Niki isn't even being Niki, that court thing has her so worked up.

Me: <3
Niki: I <3 U2

"What time are we leaving?" I ask.
"Whenever you are ready," he smiles back.

Me: Be there in 30.

Niki: K

Tossing the phone in my bag, I grab the car keys. "I'm going straight there. You following?"

"Sure am." He opens the front door and we both head out.

"Hey Kyle?"

"Yeah?"

"We. Are. Going. To. A. Carnival!" I skip down the sidewalk to the car. "Shake-ups and cotton candy and tenderloins, oh my!" I continue down the path.

"You're nuts." He shines me his dimples, following me to the car. "I love that this makes you so happy."

"You make me happy!" I start to open the door when I'm swung around, body pressed against the car.

"You make me happy, too!" He cups my face in his hands, breathing me in as his kiss promises more...*tonight*. Breaking the kiss, he says, "Now, we better get going."

"We could just stay in."

"Get in." He reaches down to swat me on the butt as he walks off.

"I was trying..."

"Be safe!" He waves his keys in the air.

"Always!" I shout back.

After dropping the car off at Niki's, Kyle got a call that someone had trespassed on one of his WilliamSon projects. Since Drew is on baby watch, Kyle volunteered to be on call for any emergencies.

Love Conquer

"This will only take a minute." He reaches behind the seat and grabs his hat and glasses. "I just need to make sure nothing has been touched."

"Can I come?"

"Sure." He reaches behind the seat again, but comes up empty-handed. "Dammit. I forgot Lee borrowed my other hat." He grabs a camera out of the console. "Next time I'll show you around."

"Don't be too long."

"I won't." He shuts the door and heads toward the house.

Not knowing what to do, I flip through the radio stations, trying to find something to distract me, when his phone begins to vibrate in the center console.

I know I shouldn't pick it up, but when I see a gorgeous blonde pop up, I can't help but wonder who she is. If I swipe now, it will answer. If I swipe later, I'll be invading his privacy.

I don't want to let the war of the hearts consume me, with my past sneaking up on my present, tainting everything that is good.

Kyle's good.

Setting the phone down, I opt to lay my seat back and relax and try to get out of my own head.

Kyle's good.

I breath slowly, remembering everything that has happened since I met him. Kyle has always been honest.

Kyle's good.

He's respected my past. Never pressured me.

Kyle's good.

His phone beeps with a text.

Kyle's good.

I'm not going to look. I'm going to let it be.

The door swings open. "Sorry it took so long." He hops in, throwing his hat in the back and glasses in the console.

"It's okay. Was anything bothered?"

"Not that I can tell, but I went ahead and called the station to have a car drive by randomly." He reaches for his phone.

"That's good news."

"What now?" He scans through his phone. He looks at me and holds up the phone. "My ex. She wants to talk."

"Oh?"

Kyle's good.

"It can wait. Today is our day."

Kyle is good and he is mine!

KYLE

OF ALL DAYS, SHE HAD to call today. I would like to say she doesn't affect me, but for some reason there is still this pull there and I'm not sure why.

Do I want her back? No. Do I wish things would have been different? Yes.

Does it get easier the more time I spend with Nina? Hell yeah. With Nina, everything is easy. I never have to second-guess my feelings. She brings out a raw emotion in me that I didn't even know existed.

She frees me from everything.

"I have to say, I'm really stuffed this time. If I eat another

Love Conquer

bite, I will explode." I hand her the bag of cotton candy.

She holds up her hand, which is coated in the crystal candy. "I need to wash these."

"Or..." I grab her wrist "I can do this." I lick every single finger clean.

"That's a great alternative."

"I thought so." I hold out my hand. "Hand hug?"

"Always."

We stroll through the carnival, playing games here and there, never winning a damn thing.

"So, tell me, what was your favorite thing about today?" Tilting my head, I watch for her reaction.

"Tonight." She waggles her eyebrows.

"Out of all the games, rides, food, fun, you are going with tonight? Something that hasn't even taken place?"

"I'm hopeful." She leans into me, putting an arm around me and holding on tight.

"Who says anything is going to happen?"

"You did." She looks up at me through her lashes, batting them. "I'm ready."

I pretend to look around. "Where's the nearest exit?" I pull us around in a circle.

"Kyle..." She's in hysterics laughing at my antics.

Finding a fence, I lean her up against it, pinning her arms above her head.

"Kyle..." Her laughing slows as her breathing speeds up.

"Tonight will be great," I agree, leaning in slow, teasing her with the promise of what is to come.

"Kyle?" A female voice behind me causes me to turn.

Shit!

"I thought that was you." She comes closer as Nina steps out from behind me, reaching for my hand.

"Who's this?" She waves her hand at Nina. "I'm Tristan, the ex." She steps forward, holding out her right hand.

Nina keeps hold of my hand, but steps forward. "I'm Nina, the girlfriend."

"Oh really? That was fast." Tristan can't help herself, throwing in a little dig that I know she hopes Nina will pick up on.

"Hey babe?" My stepbrother comes around the corner, pushing a stroller. "I couldn't find the—" He stops in his tracks, looking at the scene unfolding.

"Kyle." He nods at me.

"Jack."

"I heard you are coming to Trinity's party and bringing a guest." He pushes the stroller closer. "Is this the plus one?"

"Yes."

"Well? Aren't you going to introduce us?" He pushes the stroller closer still.

Nina squeezes my hand multiple times and I'm pretty sure it's some kind of an SOS code that I'm unable to read.

"Okay, I guess not." He holds out his hand. "I'm Jack, his stepbrother."

Nina gasps, looking between all of us.

I can't move, but I can hold on for dear life.

"That's Nina, his girlfriend," Tristian interrupts.

"That's great."

"Ky-ky!" Trinity sticks out her hands and as much as I don't want to be around her, I do. She is the reason I hate the two people standing in front of me.

Love Conquer

Forgiveness is hard, but losing a family is harder. Those two took her away from me and there is nothing I can do. She's not mine.

Squeezing my hand, Nina steps forward. "This must be the birthday girl." She reaches in and tickles Trinity's side, causing the cutest giggle to escape her lips.

Pulling Nina back, I hold her in front of me. "We better get going." I wave at Trinity. "See you soon."

"Bye-bye." She waves her tiny hands.

"See you Friday," Jack says, one hand on the stroller and one on his wife.

Walking straight past them, I don't even look back.

The family I once had is no longer mine. I just wonder how many times I'll have to tell myself this before I believe it.

Chapter 22

NINA

What just happened?

Better question, how can I protect my heart? Kyle filled it with so much hope I was soaring on cloud nine, but now I feel as if there's a leak and it's slowly deflating.

We started off with such an amazing day, the possibilities were endless. I was ready. I wanted to move our relationship to the next level, give myself to someone who would truly appreciate it.

Kyle told me he was damaged. But this? This is crazier than the "Who's on first?" comedic bit. Except there is nothing funny about it.

His ex is his sister-in-law, married to his stepbrother, and how does Trinity play into this? Is she Jack's or Kyle's?

"This isn't how I wanted to tell you," Kyle says flatly, eyes on the road.

Please, look at me.

"I know." I lean my head against the window.

"I just wanted us to have time."

Me too.

"I know." I begin to pick at my fingernails.

Love Conquer

"I was going to tell you before the party."

I need a hug.

As if he read my mind, he lays his arm across the console, palm up.

Turning in my seat, I reach out and take his hand in mine.

Squeeze.

Raising our hands to my lips, I feather light kisses across his.

"This is just us." He gives me a sideways glance. "Only us."

"I know."

"No, you don't. This right here." He brings our hands to his chest. "It's ours."

Hand hugs.

This was for me and only me. What we have isn't just a rebound. It is something, but how much of something is it? Am I only around because he can't have who he really desires? I need to know.

"Will you explain to me what happened back there? Cause honestly, I'm hoping I'm making it out to be so much more than what it really is."

His brother, his ex-wife and a child that I'm beginning to think could be his. A family he has always wanted. Stolen from him.

"Whatever you are thinking, it's probably right." He briefly looks over at me, then back to the road.

"Kyle, I have a past too." I contemplate telling him the whole story so maybe he will open up. "And I promise we will talk about it, but tonight, after this, I need to know yours."

I wait for him to pull over, but he just keeps driving.

"Tristan was my best friend growing up. She was literally

the girl next door. We never dated until high school, but man, I had the biggest crush on her. Once I started to notice girls, she was front and center." A small smile creeps across his face at the memory.

I want to be jealous, hating the woman who stole his heart so young, but I can't.

"Then when my mom married Jack's dad, he became the brother I never had. We were inseparable, making our duo a trio. He was a year older and left us behind most of the time though, forcing us together."

I don't speak, just listen, hating that this line divides his once perfect family.

"There was a time in high school, Tris and I were sophomores and Jack was a junior, when I thought maybe Jack had a crush on her, but when I brought it up, he pushed it back onto me." He shakes his head. "Said I needed to get a clue before I lost her."

"He was talking about himself," I finally say something.

"Apparently so." He nods.

"So how did you end up married?"

"Jack went away to school and we stayed local. We were easy, we connected on every level, the next step seemed like forever..."

"Do you think they were involved before you were married?" I ask the question I know will be the hardest to answer, but it's the only reason that makes sense as to why he acted the way he did back there.

"Yes." His hand grips the steering wheel so hard his knuckles are turning white. "Shortly after we were married, he came to town for a family get-together. I got called to the lumber yard for something and he told me he would take her home."

"Kyle, I'm so sorry." I squeeze his hand.

"Trinity isn't mine, if that is what you are wondering, but I thought she was," he says as he pulls into Niki's driveway.

"Wh-what are we doing here?" I begin to panic. This happened, but it doesn't mean we can't still be together. He needs me more than ever.

"I need a minute and with you not having a vehicle, I wasn't about to leave you stranded at your place." He starts to open the door, but I grab his elbow, pulling him back.

"Please, let's just go to my place. We can talk or not talk at all. I just need to be with you, know that you are going to be okay."

Shaking me off, he's out the door and around to mine and opening it. "This is for the best. Just tonight." He leans in, giving me a soft kiss on the forehead.

"Kyle, this is not us." I hop down and pull him into my arms. "You just need a hug." But he just stands there. Arms to the side.

"Nina, I—"

"No! You hug me dammit!" I reach down and wrap his arms around me, one at a time. "Please, Kyle."

"I don't want to hug you when I'm thinking about *her*."

I stumble back. One simple word shatters every promise. "Her?"

"Nina, wait! It's not—" Kyle throws his hands up in the air, then pulls at his hair.

"No!" I interrupt. "I've been you Kyle. I've been the one who wanted something that wasn't there. Give. The. Fuck. Up." I turn and walk away, holding back the sobs that are lurking beneath the surface.

"Trinity!" He calls out the name of the little girl so innocent and unaware of the turmoil she was born into. "I think about *her* all the time."

"What?" I spin around, wondering if I heard him right.

"I wanted her. I wanted a family more than I wanted life and I had it." He stalks toward me and pulls me against his chest. "She was mine then Jack stole her. I mourned her like she died, Nina. I said my goodbyes, but every time they come around it's like someone has risen from the dead."

"Kyle," I breathe.

"I just need some time to think. I need tonight."

Prying myself from his arms, I take a step back and whisper, "I wanted you to need *me*."

KYLE

AFTER PULLING INTO MY DRIVE, I sit and face the house that was meant for a family who never got to live there. Built from plans made by a man who loved with everything he was, only to leave those that he cared about behind. The rocking chairs, the house, the land...promises made to a family that were broken.

I wanted to fix it. I thought if I completed it, it would complete me.

I wanted to have a family and do all the things my dad promised, but never got to do.

I wanted to teach my son the art of craftsmanship; my daughter the way a man should treat her.

Love Conquer

I wanted to worship a wife who adored me in return.

"Goddammit!" I scream and pound the shit out of my steering wheel, hating the person I wanted to be.

I hate the hold they still have on my life.

I hate how I react whenever they are around.

But what I hate most of all is walking away from the only woman who has made me feel alive since it all went down.

All for what? Some dream I had as a kid. Some fucking dream I thought I could have.

Getting out, I slam the door and head to the house, but something catches my eye and stops me.

Tire swing.

"Fuck you!" I throw my head back and yell at the top of my lungs. "Fuck you for making me believe! Fuck you!"

Running up to the house, I swing open the door and head straight to the kitchen. I fling open drawers until I find what I'm looking for.

I stalk back down the path toward the swing, "How do you like me now?" I hold up the knife that has the power to knock it down with one swipe.

"You took my dreams." I reach out and push it with my foot. "You gave me hope and then you crushed it." I reach out, kicking it again.

"Why?" I fling my arms back and scream at the top of my lungs. "Why did you have to go?"

Out of breath, I reach for the rope, holding it in one hand. "Why couldn't you have stayed?

My face is soaked with tears I didn't know were falling.

I drop the knife to my side.

"Dad, I needed you. I still do."

"If you want someone to need *you*, I will," a soft, trembling voice says behind me.

Nina.

Looking up to the sky, I say a silent prayer.

I spin around and pick her up. She has no choice but to wrap her legs around me. Walking in circles. I cradle the back of her head in my hands, kissing her like I'm going to lose her, our mouths fused as one.

"Kyle," she breathes, pumping life back into my soul.

Slowly lowering us to the grass, I rest my forehead on hers and speak the only words I now know to be true.

"I *need* you." My confession is my therapy.

"I can't change the past, but I can help you live for the future." Nina's healing words pull me through.

I cover her with kisses. "Thank you."

"For what?"

"For not letting me push you away."

Tonight, I realized that I was searching for the family I lost a long time ago. I didn't need *her*, but I did need *him*.

Chapter 23

NINA

"Well, well, well. Look what the cat dragged in." Niki runs around the front room like she's lost her ever-loving mind.

"You okay?" I plop down on a bar stool in the kitchen.

"I can't find my keys." She's lifting up papers, looking under canisters.

"Niki." I try to get her attention.

"They gotta be here somewhere." She takes her purse and is about to empty the contents.

"I have them," I say loudly.

"What?"

"I've had your car since last weekend. Remember?" I hold out the keys for her.

"Dammit!" She yanks them from my hand. "I'm fucking losing it, Nina."

"What can I do?" I get up and go around the kitchen island. *Coffee always helps.*

Reaching into the cabinet, I grab one of her mugs.

"Get your greedy paws off my mug." Niki comes over to smack my hands.

I jerk away, protecting myself and the mug. "It's for you, you coffee whore." I hold up the mug and point to the saying on the front and grin like a Cheshire cat.

"Well in that case, carry on." She runs to the back to do God knows what.

Leaning against the counter, I break out my phone to text Kyle.

Me: I miss you already.
Kyle: Me too. Have you guys left yet?
Me: Getting ready to.
Me: You miss you already?
Kyle: Funny. I do miss the me I am when I'm with you.
Me: Good answer.
Kyle: I thought so.
Me: Well, have a great day.
Kyle: See you in a few hours.
Me: xoxo

It's been almost a week since I found out the whole truth about his family. As hard as it was for me to hear, it was harder for him to tell it.

I made a promise to him, that I would be there, that I would stand by him and help him move forward, and I meant it.

If I thought he was truly in love with Tristan I would have backed out of going, but after following him to his cabin I realized it wasn't about Tristan, or even Trinity. It was the sudden loss of his dad all those years ago.

"I hope you're ready because if we don't leave now, we are going to be late."

"Me. Sitting. Ready." I hold out her coffee for her. She grabs

Love Conquer

it and downs half of it. "You're welcome?"

"I swear there's drugs in this shit." Niki walks over to the Keurig to make a cup to go.

"It's called caffeine."

"It's called get in my belly now." She adds a little creamer to the cup while it's brewing. Always in a hurry. "Oh hey! I totally forgot."

She reaches across the island and grabs her purse. "I tried to get this fixed…" She rifles through her purse. "Here it is!"

She pulls out a cell phone with a cracked screen.

Please. Don't let it be.

"Where did you get this?" I grab the phone and try to power it up.

Dead.

"It was on your bed."

Shit!

I forgot I dumped out my bag when I was gathering up things to take to the new house.

"Did you turn it on?" I ask. Closing my eyes, I chant a little prayer.

Please be dead.

Please be dead.

Please be dead.

"Oh my God, Nina." She sighs with exasperation as she puts the final touches in her coffee. "It was on your bed. I couldn't find mine. I thought that," she points to my phone then waves her phone in my face, "was this. I wasn't snooping."

"Niki," I say very calmly. "I didn't say you were, but I need to know, did you turn it on?"

"Of course I did. I thought it was mine." She bends over

to slip on one heel and then the other. "We have to get going."

"How long was it on? Did you see—"

"Okay so maybe I read some of the messages, but only from the notifications."

"Fuck the text messages." I'm really starting to freak out. "How long was it on?"

"Nina, it's okay. Gavin didn't see them either. I saw it. Thought it was mine. It wasn't and eventually it died." She holds the door open for me to leave. "End of..."

I can't breathe. My vision is blurred. What if?

"Nina?" Niki is by my side. "You're white as a ghost." She's rubbing my back and saying something, but I can't make it out.

Brandon.

"Niki." Eyes wide, I turn to face her. "He's going to find me."

"Who?"

"He used to track me all the time." I fight back the memories. I can't fall backwards. I won't.

"Oh shit!" She takes the phone from my hands. "Okay. Okay. Let's think about this." She begins pacing. "I turned it on last Thursday, you know, the day you took overnight clothes to the new house. When it turned on it pinged like a million times with messages from Brandon, but they were all apologies. It died Saturday, or at least that is when I noticed it."

"Niki—"

"I don't think he's coming for you. In one of the texts he wished you well at school."

"Do you really think that? Because—"

"I do. He knows what town I live in. He knows you have no one else. We would be the first place he looked and he hasn't."

I want to believe her, I really do. Everything she is saying is fact, but I still can't help the uneasiness that is setting in.

"Listen, if you have the slightest doubt, we are heading up to the police station right now. Fuck court."

"Oh shit! Court!"

I grab my purse and phone and head toward the door.

"Nina?" Niki stops me. "I love you and seeing you like this is killing me. After court, we are going to the police station and filing a report. Just to be on the safe side. For peace of mind."

"Okay."

"Now that we closed this door, let's go slam mine shut."

She's right. In order to open one door, you have to shut the other. I think it's about time I said my goodbyes.

As soon as we park, we take off running for the door. "Come on, we can't be late!" Niki hollers back at me.

"Hello?" I point to the bottom of my sundress. It may be smack dab in the middle of summer, but running across the parking lot is causing a bit of wardrobe malfunction.

"What?" She turns, running backward. "Oh!" She nods and pivots back around.

I swear that woman is lying about the amount of cardio she does. There is no way someone can book it as fast as she can, wearing those things she has on her feet. No. Freakin'. Way.

"Almost there!" she shouts, taking two steps at a time.

"Hell no!" I stop dead in my tracks and take the stairs like a normal human being.

"Hurry." She waves me on.

"I'll be right behind you."

Hands on knees, I take a quick break before I take the stairs one at a time. I catch up to Niki in the security line.

"Purse, cell phones and all metal objects over here." The deputy doesn't even look up as he directs traffic.

Niki steps through first and causes the alarm to go off.

"It's probably these." Niki points to diamond studs that adorn each ear.

"Please step through and to your right." The deputy directs her to the person who is working the wand so she can be scanned from head to toe.

I step through without a problem, but when I head toward Niki, I see the deputy scanning her nether regions and Niki with her hands on her hips, looking bored.

"I'm telling you, it's a piercing." She seems irritated. "Google it."

"Miss, I'm going to have to call this in." He tilts his head to the side and radios someone.

"Niki!" I whisper loudly. "You have a piercing?"

"Yes!" she whispers back. "Why are we whispering about it?"

"Because it's down there." I point my finger toward her hoo-ha.

"Nina, I really have failed you as a sister. Like seriously."

"Miss," the deputy interrupts. "You've been cleared."

"Why, thank you, Deputy," Niki replies as she begins to take off toward the stairs.

"Are we going to talk about this?" I chase after her.

"What's there to talk about?"

"What made you do it? Is Gavin—"

"Oh, hell no! Gavin is a fucking beast in the sack." Niki

turns around to scold me for even suggesting otherwise.

"Miss Niki! Miss Niki!" A little boy comes running up. "I thought it was you."

Niki swings around. "Tucker!" She beams at the sight of him. "How have you been, buddy? Enjoying your summer?"

"Miss Niki! I've spent the summer with my dad! Can you believe that?"

At the mention of Tucker's dad, Niki goes pale.

"Tucker, buddy, I need you to stay with me." A man with the most gorgeous steely blue eyes comes running down the stairs. "Niki."

"Aiden." Niki straightens her back. "I heard you have been having an eventful summer."

"It's been an adjustment." He nods. "Listen," he looks between the two of us. "Can I talk to you for a moment?"

"Niki?" I reach out to touch her.

I don't know much about last summer, but what I do know isn't good. I tried to do some digging, but apparently Aiden Alexander has enough money to keep things out of the press.

"I'm fine." She pats my hand. "Aiden, whatever you need to say to me, you can say in front of my sister."

"Okay, just give me a second," he says, reaching into a backpack and pulling out a coloring book and crayons.

"Niki, are you sure you want to talk to him? I can faint on demand. Call security. Pretend I'm going into labor." I puff out my stomach, rubbing it for effect. "Things would be so much easier if Gavin was here."

"Okay, don't do that again. No kids until after marriage." She squints at me. "How about no sex until after marriage, too. As for Gavin? He's just running a little late. There is no way he would miss this."

"Alright. I think that should keep him busy for a couple minutes." Aiden has returned.

"What's up?" Niki takes a step back, noticeably distancing herself.

"I wanted to apologize. For everything." He looks between us again. "For not telling you that I was married. For slapping you. For what Carmen did."

"That ship has sailed, Aiden. It's too late."

"I'm in therapy now. I wanted to make sure what I did to you didn't happen to anyone else." He takes a step, lowering his voice. "I didn't mean to do it, but I was just so damn afraid of losing you, that I ended up losing control in the process."

"Aiden, I accept your apology, but I don't want you to think that if you wouldn't have raised a hand to me, that things would have worked out. I was in love with my best friend and eventually, that would have become an issue." She takes a step forward this time. Her confession gives her the closure she has needed.

"Thank you." His smile is forced.

"I can tell you love Tucker, and that is enough for me. You stepping up and taking charge speaks volumes."

"Niki, he is the greatest thing. I hate that they hid him from me all this time." He shakes his head. "I've missed out on so much."

"Aiden, we need you in here." A younger man comes walking up, probably one of his attorneys.

"I'm coming."

He reaches out his hand to Niki and she takes it. "You changed my life. Made me see that there is more out there.

Thank you."

"Goodbye, Aiden." Niki gives his hand a shake before she pulls it free. "Let's Judge Judy this thing." She laughs.

"Yes, let's do it."

Seeing Niki talk to Aiden makes me realize that sometimes in order to move on from the past you have to face it. Running away is a fix, but not a solution.

Goodbye, Brandon.

Chapter 24

KYLE

"Kyle, I'm so nervous. What if they don't like me?" Nina turns to me, placing her hand on my chest right before we make it to the front door.

"Stop worrying your bottom lip." I lean over and give her a small kiss. "That's my job." I wink.

"Great. Now I'm all horny and I have to meet your parents." Her emerald eyes shine with desire.

"Let's go." I grab her hand and start to tug her back toward the truck.

"Kyle!" She digs in her heels. "If we leave, they will really hate me."

"I'm kidding," I laugh.

"There you guys are." My mom comes out the door and heads straight for Nina. "Oh my! You must be Nina! I have heard *so* much about you." Mom pulls her in for a hug.

"You have?" Nina looks up and flashes me a smile.

"Of course, my dear. Just the other day he was telling me about taking you to—"

"Mom!" I scold. "That's supposed to be a surprise."

"Well, my dear, it's a good one." She grabs Nina's hand

and pulls her inside. "I'm Brenda." She looks around for my stepdad. "Jimmy!"

"Yes, honey?" He comes around the corner.

"Jimmy? This is Kyle's Nina!" My mom twirls her around. "Isn't she gorgeous?"

Reaching over, I take Nina's hand and twirl her right back to my arms. "Nina, if you haven't figured it out, this is my mom, Brenda, and my stepdad, Jimmy Bennett."

"Nonsense. You can call us Mom and Dad."

"Jimmy? Mom been into the Bloody Marys again?" I clap him on the back as I walk Nina to the back of the house where I assume Jack and his family are.

"Kyle William Lewis! That was one time!" She holds up her finger. "One! And you *still* won't let me live that down."

"Well Brenda, it was pretty damn funny," Jimmy chimes in.

"Ky-Ky!" Trinity runs up to me, grabbing hold of my leg.

"What's up squirt?" I bend down to give her a little tickle. "Is it your birthday?"

"Uh-huh!" She looks up at me with the same eyes her mom used to. "Pwezence!"

"Come here." I pick her up, giving her a little toss in the air and catching her. "Nina here has a present for you."

That's all it takes. Just the mention of presents and Trinity is holding out her arms to go to Nina.

Nina looks over at Tristan and Jack on the couch and back to me, unsure what to do.

"It's okay." I lean Trinity over for Nina to take her. "Trin, can you say Nina?"

"Pwetty." She rubs a hand over Nina's long, dark hair, then leans in and snuggles her neck.

"I think you're pretty, too." Nina taps her nose.

"Looks like someone is getting sleepy." Tristan moves from the couch and comes over to take Trinity. "How about a nap before we open presents?"

"Mmm-no!" Trinity shakes her head and holds on to Nina. "My Nema." She tries to get out Nina's name.

"Ohhhhh! Is little miss Trinity giving her momma a hard time?" My mom comes strolling in to save the day.

"Uh-uh." Trinity shakes her head wildly.

"Come to Memaw, birthday girl." She reaches out and Trinity goes straight to her.

"I'll just put her down in our bedroom."

"Thanks, Mom," Tristan replies.

"So, did you guys happen to bring any fireworks?" I walk over to take a seat in the oversized chair by Jack.

"Fuck you, Kyle." He laughs.

I pull Nina down next to me and she curls into my side.

"Jack loves fireworks." I give him a hard time. "Was it roman candles that were your favorite?" I hold a finger up to my chin, pretending to think.

Tristan walks up and takes a seat beside Jack. "You're confused. He loves the sparklers. You know, the long wire ones."

"Screw those damn things." Jack shivers.

Turning to Nina, I say, "See, Jack and I decided that this one over here," I jab my thumb in Tristan's direction, "needed to have a birthday to remember. So, we spent the afternoon making a mess in Mom's kitchen while attempting to make a cake for her fifteenth birthday."

"It was one to remember for sure." She laughs at the memory.

"Of course, when it came time to surprise her, we couldn't

find any candles. Jack had the bright idea of using leftover sparklers from the Fourth of July."

"Oh no! Tell me he didn't," Nina groans.

"Oh yes! He did." Tristan slaps him on the knee as Jack rubs his right brow.

"I was supposed to carry the cake. You know, since she was my girlfriend." I slide in a little dig.

"It was my idea to make it," Jack bites back, pulling Tristan into his side.

"Anyway, this sucker here sticks the sparklers in the cake, and then lights them." I throw my head back and laugh at the memory. "I pick up the cake to carry it, but Jack lifts it out of my hands and right into his face." I get up and act out the scene. "Burning. Off. His. Eyebrows. Like gone. Completely."

"True story." Jack nods. "I had senior pictures the next day, too."

"Noooooooo!" Nina gasps. "What did you do?"

"Skipped them."

"Ohhhhhh. I bet Jimmy was upset," Nina chuckles.

"Yeah, I may have been grounded for a couple weeks." Jack leans forward, finger in the air. "But, it worked with my skipping school story."

"Check this out." I lean forward, hands clasped together. "He paid the old man down the road to call the school and tell them he was sick with mono, and to send all his lessons home with me." I stand, walk over to Jack and hold out my fist. "Bro? That was epic."

"Dude, I was the shit." He bumps my fist.

And for the first time in a few years, I feel good. Like I have my family back.

"You know, this has been a pretty good day," Nina says as she walks up to me and hands me a beer.

"So, you're not going to run for the hills?" I wrap my arm around her, watching Trinity play with her presents.

"I think you're stuck with me, Kyle." She steps in front of me, standing on her tiptoes to give me a kiss.

"Mmm! I don't know what I did to deserve you." I pull her in closer.

"I could say the same," she smiles back.

"Kyle!" My mom peeks her head out the back. "Can you tell Jimmy that we cannot paint this room golden yellow? It's hideous."

"Nina is an interior designer," Beer in hand, I raise it up and point my finger down. "I bet she would love to give some input."

She slaps me on the chest. "I'm not," she argues.

"You very well could be, if you wanted to." I grin. "You are *that* good."

"Nina, can you come help me and Tristan for a second?" Mom asks.

"I'll be back in a few." She bends down. "Hey, birthday girl? You want to come with me and Memaw?"

"Go bye-bye." Trinity makes grabby hands at Nina.

"No bye-bye." She laughs, then grabs Trinity. "Let's go see what Memaw is doing. Be back in a few."

A week ago, today would have been a disaster. Family events, for me, were only attended out of obligation. It would have been a day of awkward, tension-filled conversations, but today feels like the home I used to know.

Family.

Scanning the yard, I see it's just me and Jack. Even though we come from different parents, that man was a brother in every sense of the word. I would have given the roof over my head, shirt off my back, a kidney...fuck if I wouldn't have given my life for my brother, but him? He took not just my pride, but my *world*.

Finally, after all this time, with Nina's help, I realize that sometimes what we want isn't exactly what we need. The way I feel when I'm around her makes me know those words are true.

It's either now or never. I need to take all those feelings, bottle them up and throw them out to sea. Because today felt so damn good.

"Well, Jack, I guess it's just us." I walk over to him and clink bottles.

"I guess it is." He nods for me to take the seat beside him.

"Hey, there's something I need to talk to you about." Jack turns in his seat to face me.

Scratch that. Maybe today isn't the day. Him saying those words, *"I need to talk to you,"* brings the past up front and center. I've heard those words countless times over the years and today I still don't want to have the talk.

"Man, if it has to do with Tristan—"

"It does, but I need to get this off my chest." He stands and starts to pace.

Shit!

"Off your chest? A confession?" I snap.

"Kyle, man, I just need you to listen to me for once." He throws his head back in exasperation.

He's the one who stole my life and I'm the one who's wearing him out? Fuck that.

"Don't do it. Today has been a step forward. Let's not take a step back."

"Today has been great, but man, the way you look at me?" Jack comes to stand in front of me. "It kills me."

"Shit! You really want to go there?"

"I *need* to go there," he confirms.

"Jack, it's your daughter's birthday. Not today."

"I know when my daughter's birthday is and honestly, this shit has to end so we can move on," he spits back.

"I wasn't really sure if you could remember or not. You know, since you bailed that weekend, leaving me to basically deliver Trinity in the backseat of my truck." I slam my beer down and shove my hands in my pockets to keep myself from knocking the shit out of him.

"Fuck you! I didn't know! I fucking didn't know. If I did, I would have been there. *I* would have been the one holding her hand, helping her through anything and everything," he barks.

I jump up. "What do you want from me? I'm doing the best I can. You're my brother, Jack. My fucking brother." I spin around, taking a step forward.

"It's not what you think. I've tried to explain, but you never listen."

That does it. *Never listen?* How can you listen to someone who has never tried to be heard?

"You want this? You want to do this now? Today of all days?" I'm in his face. Pissed. My body is boiling over in anger. "Of course you do." I nod.

"I never meant for it to happen the way it did." He bows his head in defeat.

Is he for real right now?

"The way it did? The way it did?" My hands are on his chest, shoving him backwards before I can get control of myself. "So, you didn't care that it fucking happened? You just care about the *way* it happened?"

"I deserve that." He regains his balance and takes a step forward.

"Jack, you slept with my wife, got her pregnant and then let me claim her as my own." I run a hand over my face. "You let me love Trinity when you knew. You *knew*, man."

"I didn't."

"You're a fucking liar!" I scream back at him, not caring if they can hear us inside. "You fucked my wife. The moment you stuck your dick in her is the moment you could have very well been her dad."

"That's not fair." He shakes his head. "This isn't how I planned for this to go down."

"Well, *I* fucking didn't plan for you to *steal* my whole family." My next words are laced with venom. "Was that your plan all along? Your mom dies so you need mine? Slowly weave your way into my life and get to experience the life I had growing up? Your dad—"

"You bastard!" He lunges at me. Hands under my arms, he tries to tackle me to the ground, but the days of him being bigger and stronger are over.

"What?" I shove him off me. "It hurts to have someone degrade what you once had, doesn't it?" I start to walk away.

"My mom and dad weren't like yours, but they loved each other." He shouts after me. "I didn't *need* yours, but what I did need was a brother, a friend."

"You sure as hell have a funny way of showing it." I whip around.

"Kyle, I swear to God, on my family, I never meant for any of this to happen!" He holds his arms out wide.

"Your family? That was *my* family. Mine!" I close my eyes tight, trying to block out the last few years. "I loved her since she was the freckle-faced, pig-tailed girl living across the street. I was there when she got her first B, her first bad haircut, first pimple, I was there when those guys started the rumors, I took her to every dance and walked her home every day. I loved her! *My* family."

"I loved her too," he says quietly.

"You what?" I hold a hand up to my ear.

Is he saying those words? *Now*?

"I loved her too." We are chest to chest. "It was because I loved *you* that I knew I couldn't love *her*. My brother..." He holds his hand to his heart. "And hurting you wasn't an option."

"You didn't just hurt me. You fucking *destroyed* me!"

"Kyle, man?" he pleads.

Drawing back, I let it go. Not once, but twice. Drawing blood.

Stop!

His head flies back. "Fuck!" he roars, his face now soaked with blood. He lunges for me again, shoving me back.

Stop!

"I loved her and if you would have opened your eyes..." Another shove. "You would have seen that she felt the same way, but you..." One more, and I begin to stumble as the words come flying out of his mouth. "Were too fucking selfish to even

Love Conquer

notice." I fall backwards.

Please stop!

"Kyle!" Jack's eyes widen as he reaches for me.

Losing my footing, I stumble back, knocking something over. As I spin around I see it's not something, but someone. *Nina!*

"Nina!" I'm down and beside her as soon as she hits the ground.

"No-no-no-no-no-no-no-no!" She's on her back, scooting away. From *me*.

Leaning over, I reach for her to pull her to me. "Let me help you up, baby. I didn't mean to—" I stand up, trying to help right her, but fear laces her face.

Fear of me!

"Get away from me." She holds up a hand.

"Nina—"

"I yelled for you to stop. You wouldn't," she interrupts. She's looking directly at me, but something's missing. Her face is empty, the love for me vanishing in a moment.

"Baby, I didn't mean to—" I reach down to grab her arm.

"I said don't touch me." She jerks her elbow away.

"Kyle, maybe just give her a minute." Jack is beside me, pulling me back.

Wrenching my arm out of his grasp, I spin to look at him. "You knew she was back there. Is this what you wanted?" I push him. "It wasn't enough you took my family, but now you want to ruin my future?"

"I don't know." He shakes his head. "I mean, I don't know how long she was there. I only saw her going down."

"Screw you." I turn back around.

Falling to my knees, I'm back at her side. "Nina, it's me," I whisper. "Look right here. Just me and you, *always*."

"Let me help you get her up."

"You don't lay a fucking hand on her. Do you understand?" I warn, twisting around, glaring up at him. Jack looks just as worried as I am.

"You got this, Nina. Come back to me."

Her face turns to mine. Her mouth opens, then shuts.

"Nina, let me do something," I plead.

"Take me home then." She stands up, brushing herself off. "Now."

"What's all the commotion out here?" My mom comes storming out, catching site of Nina. "Oh, dear!" She looks between us. "Are you okay sweetie?"

Nina looks humiliated. Standing next to her, I wrap my arm around her shoulders. This time she lets me. "Mom? Nina isn't feeling too well. I'm going to take her home," I say as I walk her past my family, through the house, and out to my truck.

Opening the door, I try to help her up, but she smacks my hand away. Not knowing what else to do, I round the truck and hop in, putting it into drive. She wants to go home, but I can't give her that. If I can't help her, maybe Niki can.

Laying my hand on the center console, I turn my hand over, palm up. I wait for her to accept the offer and put her hand in mine.

My apology.
My comfort.
But it never comes.

Chapter 25

NINA

The more I try to deal on my own, the more I begin to fade away. The darkness lingers in front of me each and every day, and I usually walk away, but today it caught up with me.

Consuming.

"I feel so stupid." I cry on Niki's shoulder.

"Don't do this Nina. You have nothing to feel stupid about." She cradles my head as she rocks us back and forth.

"I knew it was an accident, but the moment I saw the anger inside of him, I froze. I saw him falling backwards." I let the sobs rack my body. "I couldn't move. I couldn't see who was really in front of me. I only saw *him*."

"Shhhh...it's okay, sweetie." She pulls my head back. "You didn't do this."

"Didn't I?" I swipe my tears away and get up. "I didn't leave. I stayed."

I stayed.

"Nina?" She comes up beside me.

"It's true." I begin pacing the room. "I stayed and let his actions destroy me. His words kill me. His fists mark me."

"Don't you dare! Don't you dare say those words." Niki is

in front of me, pleading with me to listen. "Don't you *believe* those words."

"I don't want to, but then there are times like today..." I look up, trying to fight back a fresh flood of tears. "That I feel weak and helpless. If I could have just..."

"Nina, honey...you *have* to talk to someone. Living like this is not an option. It's destroying you," she says as she reaches up to brush the tears away.

"I thought I was doing good." I shake my head, curling my lips in. "Each day, I picked myself up piece by piece. I was finding myself, who I am now. But today..." I wipe my eyes, but there are no more tears. "I was held captive by the nightmares."

"Nina..."

"Niki? Will I ever be whole again? Will I *ever* be able to live a life without *him*?"

"Yes, my sweet girl. I promise you that." She pulls me back in for a hug and the tears I thought were gone come flooding back.

"How?"

"Let those who love you in. Me, Gav, we are here for you, and Kyle."

"Kyle?"

"Girl, that man is worthless without you. I thought I was going to have to pick him up and carry him in when he dropped you off."

"What?"

"After I saw you walk through those doors, I went outside to give him a piece of my mind, but Nina, he looked just as broken as you." She goes to stand by the window, pulling back the curtain. "He was scared, and a fear like that only comes from losing someone you love."

Love?

"How do you—"

"I've been there. I have been him and I've seen him." She turns, letting the curtains fall closed. "Gavin and I, we've had a rough road, but the one thing that got us through was being there to pick each other up."

"How do I love him back?" I stand, head down, feeling defeated.

"You let them in here." She taps her chest. "It's a fucking battle, the war of hearts, but..." She reaches down, taking my hand in hers, and squeezes.

Hand hug.... Kyle.

"Sometimes to conquer love, you have to battle your past. Nina, go to war. Fight the battle and win."

Her words sink in. I have been so afraid to show my heart that I have basically given up before we could ever start.

"Nina, take me home."

I survived Brandon, but I won't survive losing him.

I refuse to be another victim. The past is a disease, threatening to infect my future. Nope. I'm not doing it. Today, I'm making a choice. I'm going to be a survivor.

Leaving was the first step. Saying goodbye will be the second, closing the door on everything that sucked the life from me.

I will stand once again, calling to the light and flipping off the dark.

Hearing a light rap on the door, I pull my robe tight and

pad my way to see who it is.

Taking a deep breath, I close my eyes.

You are not hopeless!

Opening the door, I see a man once tall and strong slumped over in defeat.

I did this.

"Kyle." His name falls from my lips.

He lifts his head and swallows. "Can I come in?"

Nodding, I open the door wider.

Inviting.

"Nina, I'm so, so sorry." He turns to pull me into his arms, but stops.

I did this. I caused him to pull back. To doubt himself.

"I don't know what happened back there, but what I do know is that I'm not going to lose you."

"You haven't lost me," I whisper.

"I'm not going to let you run away without a fight." He begins to pace. "You came into my life and took my shattered heart and pieced it back together..." He stops. "Wait, what?"

"You haven't lost me," I repeat.

"Oh, thank God!" He stalks toward me, pulling me into his arms.

I tense.

He's not Brandon.

He squeezes harder.

Kyle.

I relax.

"Kyle, I'm so broken—"

"Everyone is a little broken." He steps back and looks down at me. "But I need you to trust me with the cracks. Let me be

Love Conquer

the one to repair you, while you heal me."

"You don't understand." I turn my back to him.

He comes up behind me, wrapping his arms around my waist.

I tense.

"What did I do?" He backs away. "I swear..."

I turn to face him and our eyes connect.

"I'm not that person," he continues. "I would never lay a hand on you." He sticks his hands in his pockets.

"I know you wouldn't—"

"Then let me in," he interrupts.

I want to. I so desperately do, but there is something that is keeping me from doing so. Is it me? Is it Brandon?

"You don't understand!" I shout. "Being with me..." I shake my head. "It won't be easy. I would be lying if I said days like today would never happen again."

"Nina, I can't understand if you don't tell me." He begs for any answer I'm willing to give.

"How do I tell you? How do I admit I'm *weak*?" I'm all over the place, nervous that once he finds out, he'll leave.

"Nina? You aren't weak, baby." He comes over and slowly turns me around, being cautious about touching me. "You," he cups my face, "are so fucking strong."

Laughing, I break free.

"Oh really? Is that why I dropped out of school and let a man, whom I thought loved me, control everything?" I begin to count off on my fingers. "House, money, bills, what I wore, what I ate, how I ate..." The tears start to flow. "So strong that I sat at home while he worked late nights, screwing his way to the top? So damn strong that I hid going to design school, afraid that he would get upset? So fucking strong that I cowed down when he raised a hand?"

I bend over to catch my breath, exhausted from the confession.

Hands on my knees, I look up at him through my lashes. "Kyle, that isn't strong. That's weak." I stand tall and turn to the mirror that we hung the other day. "I wasn't just afraid of Brandon, I was terrified of myself." I take a step closer and even though you can't see the marks, I know the scars are there. "I'm my own kind of monster."

"Nina." He stands behind me, his reflection staring at mine. "My sweet Nina, full of strength and scars."

"I'm hopeless."

"Take my hand." He holds out his hand, palm up.

Turning, I take it.

He squeezes. "I still need you."

"Kyle the thing about my scars, they're like demons within, never playing by the rules. Some days I'm able to push them down, but days like today," I tap my temple, "they just fight harder to get in here."

"Then let me in there." He holds our hands over my heart. "So I can heal here." He leans over, kissing my temple.

"I don't know. When I give up control, when I turn away, the demons always stay."

"Nina, let *me* stay. Let me be the one to protect you, to fight the battles of your heart, saving you from the war. Let me *love* you." And on a desperate plea he confesses what we both already know.

"I."

"Love."

"You."

Kyle is so real, his words raw, hitting home. I let the walls fall back down.

"I love you too." I confess. Taking his other hand, I whisper a plea. "Kyle, take me. My pain, my fear."

He pulls me to him and rests his forehead against mine as the tears start to fall. We stand for what could be forever. I lose all sense of time when he holds me. As always, he takes his time with me, lets me set the pace.

I said everything I could with my words. And what I couldn't say is now falling from my eyes, washing away the hurt, the past.

I feel his thumbs brushing my cheeks, and the whisper of his lips begins to flutter across my face. His kisses grow more urgent and my mouth finds his, licking the seam of his lips and he opens up and deepens the kiss.

We communicate with our mouths.

Kissing.

Tasting.

Giving.

Taking.

He groans against my mouth and my body instinctively presses into him, needing to be closer.

Taking the hint, he lifts me into his arms, and I hold on tight as he carries me back to my bedroom. As he sits me down at the foot of bed he slides my body down his.

Catching my breath, I watch him watching me. Taking my

hands in his, he squeezes. "Nina, we don't have to rush this."

Who knew a hand hug could be foreplay?

Every squeeze of his palm shoots straight to my core and I know that I'm tired of waiting.

"We're not. Kyle, please."

Freeing my hands, I untie my robe, letting it fall to the floor before placing a hand on either side of his face and bringing his mouth back to mine.

Kiss.

"I want this."

Kiss.

"I want you."

Kiss.

"I need you."

Kiss.

"Don't make me..." he interrupts me and seals his mouth over mine as he backs me up and lays me beneath him on the bed.

When he climbs between my legs, I feel his arousal pressed between my thighs and I rock into him, closing my eyes tightly.

"Nina, Nina look at me." And the doubt creeps in. But opening my eyes is all it takes to erase the doubts, the fear of rejection, because I see his desire immediately.

"I don't want to rush this," he says. "I want to savor you, the way you were meant to be savored." He draws my tank over my head and I lift my arms to help him rid me of the barrier, slowly dragging the lace up my arms. "I'm going to worship you with my hands, my mouth, and my body."

Speechless.

Leaning forward he traces the curve from my shoulder

to neck, and moisture floods my center in anticipation of his mouth being someplace else.

Everywhere he puts his mouth it's like a healing touch. Every kiss, every swipe of the tongue, every gesture, every word... he's putting me back together.

His hand moves lower, pulling my pajama bottoms to the side, and he drags his finger through my sex, back and forth.

Back. And. Forth.

He places delicate kisses on my thighs while he continues pleasuring me. I rock against his hand, wanting more.

"Kyle. Now. Please." I begin to buck as he picks up the pace.

"Not until you come for me." His voice is heavy with lust. And I lose it, crying out as an orgasm tears through me.

Once again, our mouths find each other. His hands roam my body, massaging as they go.

I sit up, reach for him and pull his shirt over his head.

I smile, licking my lips.

He nods, stepping back from the bed and ridding himself of jeans and boxers.

Before he climbs back to me, he reaches into his jeans pocket and pulls out a condom.

"Safety first," we say in unison, smiling.

He settles back between my legs and I feel his hard length pressed up against me as he strokes himself.

I reach down, placing my hand over his, and feel him. A hiss escapes his lips. "Nina, baby, I would love nothing more than to have your hands on me. But I need to be inside you."

Lying back, I nod and wrap my arms around his neck as he sheaths himself. I'm getting close to being ready again, just from the feel of him so close to my center.

He lines himself up and questions me once more, with just a look. "I'm yours, Kyle."

And he gently slides into me, taking his time. Our eyes lock and as he fills my body, he's also filling my heart.

"It's like you were made for me." He moans as he quickens his pace.

Our lips connect, his hands on me and mine tangle in his hair. We move as one.

My movements grow more frantic as he grows harder inside of me. Without warning, my orgasm crashes though my body and his follows right after. The only sounds are our breathing and moans as pleasure overtakes us both.

We ride out the high, and he rolls over on his back, taking me with him. I'm thankful he doesn't want to break the connection either.

Kyle takes my palm in his, giving it a squeeze, and continues holding me to him. Our hands hugging, resting on his chest, over his heart.

In this moment, I know what it is to be cherished. What we just did was beyond sex. What we have, what we can be, is more than I ever imagined I could have.

In my world, love hurts. But his touch right now is perfect. Painless.

Chapter 26

KYLE

"Are you watching me sleep?" Nina, still drowsy, opens one eye and looks up at me. "Cause that's kind of creepy. Maybe even slightly stalkerish."

Reaching under the sheets, I tickle the spot I know will make her squirm.

"Stop!" she squeals, wiggling around.

"Take it back!" I demand, continuing my assault and enjoying the fact that every little tickle causes her to rub against me in all the right places.

"Okay, okay." She throws her hand over me, brushing up against me. "Oh my." She blushes.

"Rise and shine." I wink.

"Hmmm! I have a feeling it's going to be a great morning!" She begins to stretch against my body.

She puts an arm against either side of my face. I turn my head to place a kiss against her skin, taking a moment to breathe her in.

"I just..." She stretches again, leaning against me until she's rolled herself on top of me.

"Nice move."

"I thought so," she says with a wicked grin.

Rising up on her knees, she reaches down to find what she needs and slowly takes me in, one glorious inch at a time. She closes her eyes, throwing her head back, as if I'm her drug and she just got her fix.

"Nina," I groan. "Safety first."

I don't want this feeling to end, being inside of her, no barriers. "Nina, condom." I moan, the feel of her making me lose all thoughts, all control.

"Shh." She places a finger over my lips. "I get it, safety first." She picks up the pace and now I'm the one throwing my head back.

Faster.

Harder.

"Shit, Nina!" I'm about to explode. "Condom now!" I open my eyes wide, grabbing her hips, ready to move her off.

Not missing a beat, she places her hands over mine.

"I'm."

Faster.

"On."

Harder.

"The."

Faster.

"Pilllllllllll!" Nina screams out her release, while she rides out mine.

Collapsing on top of me, keeping us connected, she smiles. "Best. Morning. Ever."

"I think I can do better." I roll us over, making sure it's a morning neither one of us will forget.

Love Conquer

♡

NINA

"Hurry up!" I holler to Kyle, who is obviously dragging from our little morning workout session.

"You were practically jumping out of a moving vehicle. Nothing safe about that, Nina!" he yells after me.

"Sorry! I need coffee, like stat." I reach the door, but Kyle's muscled arm reaches over my head to grab the door.

"Chivalry isn't dead, Nina." He opens the door wide for me to go through. "We are getting you a coffee machine after we leave here."

"Aw. Someone tired?" I look back over my shoulder, giving him my best pouty face.

"Tired?" He stands up taller, puffing out his chest. "Of course not. I could have gone a few more rounds," he says, walking past me.

"Oh really?" I stand, hands on hips.

Turning around, he stalks back up to me, pulling me into his arms. "There will never be a day I wouldn't want you." He leans down for a kiss.

"Screw it. Let's just go get the machine now." I spin around to head out the door when I see someone out of the corner of my eye and my breath catches in my throat.

Her. It's now or never.

"Nina, what's wrong?" I feel Kyle's hand on my shoulder.

"Just give me a minute." I reach up and pat his hand.

I'm not sure what I'm going to do, or what I'm going to

say. I just know I have to see for myself that she is okay. Being a prisoner of abuse is no way to live.

As I get closer, I try to search for the words that will convince her to leave. Words that show her a stranger cares...understands.

"Excuse me." I stand at the end of their table. "Hi. I know you don't know me." I scan her face. "I just wanted to let you know, that I know." I give her a minute to register what I'm saying. "I know and you aren't alone." I reach out, touching her hand. "I promise. If you want to leave, I'll help you. I'll get you the protection you need.

"You little bitch," her boyfriend spits out, coming up from behind. "Who do you think you are, coming in here and saying that? Don't think I don't notice the way you look at her."

Bingo!

"Really, I'm fine." Her eyes plead with me while she looks between the two of us.

"Penny, don't talk to her." He steps forward and she flinches.

"What's going on over here?" Kyle walks up, standing in between me and the asshole.

"Your little girlfriend is putting her fucking nose in something that has nothing to do with her."

"I'm serious...Penny, is it?" I step around Kyle to get to her. "I know it's more than the faded bruises. I see the scars you try to hide."

"Leave her alone!" The guy pushes Kyle out of the way and grabs hold of Penny's elbow.

"Man, wrong move." Kyle yanks the asshole back by the collar. "Learn to keep your hands to yourself.

"What's wrong with you people? Your little bitch—" He's interrupted when Kyle picks him up by the front of his shirt and slams him against the opposite wall.

"Someone call the police!" He squirms under Kyle's grip.

"Yes, someone call the police!" Kyle agrees. "Time's up, fucker."

"Penny, my name is Nina." I hold out my hand.

"Hi, Nina." She rejects my hand and offers up a wave.

"Can we talk outside away from this?" I plead.

She nods, her gaze never leaving the asshole's until she hits the door. The moment the door shuts behind her, her breathing picks up. Faster and faster, her eyes wide.

"Penny, look at me." I stand in front of her trying to catch her gaze. "Just look at me. Right here." I point between our eyes.

"In. Out."

See my mouth.

"In. Out."

Follow me.

"In. Out."

"I'm so scared." She pants out between breaths.

"It's scary, but I need to know...does he hurt you?"

Nodding frantically, her body is racked with sobs. At this moment, the cops pull in.

"Listen, Penny. This is where you have to make a choice and it's going to be one of the hardest things you ever do in your life." I reach out for her hand. This time she takes it. Giving it a little squeeze, I say, "Do you want to leave? No more hiding. No more pain."

"Yes," she whispers.

"Sir!" I call out to one of the police officers. "We have a domestic dispute.

"Penny, I promise, everything is going to be okay."

Chapter 27

NINA

"You know that bouncer I told you about, Shapiro?"

Niki called to give me an update on Penny, the girl from Java Talk.

"I don't think I've met him," I reply.

"Well, he is this badass who works the VIP section at Spotlight. Shapiro knows people who know people," she continues. "He's going to hide Penny until her boyfriend is found."

"Oh good." I pause to say a silent little prayer.

Even though the police were called to Java Talk, there was nothing they could do. He didn't physically assault her, nor were there signs of abuse. Just a girl and her accusations and a guy who denied them. Unfortunately, it's a flaw in the system that makes it harder for victims to be heard and feel safe after coming forward.

"Just know she is taken care of and everything is going to be okay. She's doing better."

"I don't know what to say," I tell her, and I truly don't. Everyone has come together to make sure the girl in the coffee shop has a place to survive.

Love Conquer

"You don't have to say any—" She stops talking mid-sentence.

"Niki?"

"Oh hey! Aubrey just texted that she is having contractions. I'm going to give her a call back. Watch my tweets, #babywatch."

"Give her my best, but you better keep me updated. You know I don't tweet."

"Peace out!" she hollers before hanging up.

Tucking my phone in the pocket of my robe, I head to the kitchen table to grab my glass of wine, a book and some of the new bubble bath Kyle bought me.

After the last couple of days, he thought I should take some time to wind down, so that's what I'm going to do.

I can't help but do a little dance and sing at the top of my lungs as I head down the hall to the bathroom. This living alone thing is kinda cool. Then again, Kyle has been spending the last couple of nights here, which is almost like having the best of both worlds.

Speaking of which, my phone vibrates and lights up my robe. I smile when I pull it out of my pocket and see who it is.

Kyle.

Kyle: We may have to cancel tonight. Have to work late.

Kyle: Aubrey is having contractions. Drew is heading home in a bit.

Me: I heard. Do you think she will have it tonight?

Kyle: Aubrey doesn't think so, but Drew wants to get home.

Kyle: Want me to bring home dinner?

Home.

Me: Sure. I'm just going to take a bath.

235

I set the phone on the counter and run the water. I pour in a little of the bubble bath and wait for it to suds up before I hop in.

Kyle: Using some of that stuff?
Kyle: You still there?

Hearing the series of pings, I disrobe and grab the phone off the counter, then get in the tub one step at a time.

Me: Yeah. Just running water.
Kyle: I should be home in a few hours.

Taking out the phone, I snap a selfie of me covered in bubbles and send it to him.

Kyle: Okay, make it a couple hours.
Kyle: An hour.
Kyle: Damn job.
Me: Love you.
Kyle: Love you, too.

Smiling, I lay the phone down on the bath mat and just relax. I think about the last few weeks and how things have changed. How *I've* changed. I've done things in the past month that I wasn't allowed to do for the past few years.

Closing my eyes, I let myself dream about my life and how one certain guy helped me turn it around.

For the first time in a long time, I have a job, friends and a boyfriend who lets me set the pace. Whenever I was ready, he let me surrender so we could surrender to each other and find our peace.

Love Conquer

Kyle Lewis, the hot guy no one wanted. Well, I do, and each and every day he shows me why he's perfect for me. Why he is the *only* choice for me.

He's built my confidence by encouraging me to take a few interior design courses. He's even suggested I help with a special project that he is working on with Drew — flipping a rundown subdivision. He thinks I can stage the homes for quicker sales. This man is everything I never knew I wanted.

I'm not sure how long I've been soaking, but given the water temperature is almost too cold and my hands are like prunes, I'm thinking about an hour or so.

Standing up, I almost trip, when the sound of the door slamming startles me.

"Kyle?" I call out.

Looking at the time, I see I have two missed messages.

Kyle: The guys are hauling ass. Be home sooner than later.

Kyle: It's going to be a pizza kind of night.

Sliding on a pair of panties, I throw on my robe, and quickly brush my teeth. Then I give myself a once over before I surprise my man.

Tying up my hair, I let my robe hang open and head out, doing my best catwalk down the hall.

"I see the pic worked," I announce myself, but come to a complete stop when I see the room is completely dark and the curtains are closed. "Kyle?"

No answer.

Noticing a cell phone light up, I smile and tiptoe around to face the couch.

"Hey you."

"Nina."
My blood runs cold.

KYLE

"Drew, you better get the hell out of here before your wife has your baby without you." I slap him on the back.

Aubrey called earlier and said she was having contractions but not to hurry home. Then a few minutes ago, she called with news that her water broke and Niki was running her to the hospital.

"I'm heading out now." He grabs his keys and walks over to the white board. "We need to make sure we stain these beams." He points up to the ceiling. "Then prep the room for the drywall tomorrow."

"Man, get out of here. I got this under control." I give him a little shove out the door.

"I know. I know." He turns back to me. "It's just been awhile. I'm…"

"Nervous?" I pat him on the back. "It's the good kind. Go, be with Aubrey."

"Thanks man." Drew takes off.

Picking up the radio, I call to the guys and check in to see where everyone is at and make sure we are on schedule for the day so we all can cut out early.

"I forgot my keys." Drew comes running back in, without his hardhat.

Love Conquer

"Hat!" I bark.

"I forgot it in the truck. Just grabbing my keys." He holds them up.

Walking over to him, I take my hat off and place it on top of his head. "Can't have something happen to this noggin." I knock on it. "Aubrey would kill me if something happened to you today."

He nods and smiles. "Don't be too much longer."

"Yeah, I'm right behind you. I just wanna make sure these support beams are locked in snug before I shut down for the night."

"Safety first. I got it man. Thanks for everything."

Drew starts to walk away as I knock on the makeshift wood support beams.

Solid.

Solid.

Creaking.

That's weird.

I look up and do a double-when I see one of the beams coming down. I scan the room, and see Drew at the other end. The end that's collapsing.

"Drew! Watch out!" I yell as I jump back, hoping we're both clear of the beam falling from the cathedral ceiling.

Crash.

Darkness.

Chapter 28

NINA

"What's wrong? Not happy to see me?" Brandon sits on the couch, head buried in his phone.

I hurry and secure my robe as I back away.

"H-How did you...?" I look around and see nothing is broken.

"The door." He finally looks up. "What kind of man do you take me for, Nina?"

"It was locked." I replay my motions in my head. It was locked, I know it. I always lock the door.

"Was it? Or maybe you're too preoccupied these days?" He begins to look through his phone. "It's a shame you know." He starts going through pictures of me, from older ones to more current.

I can't let him get in my head with his games. I'm no longer a component. I'm done!

"You just up and let yourself go like this." He gets up and comes to stand in front of me. "How much weight have you put on? Five, ten pounds?" He tries to reach in my robe, but I smack his hand away.

"You were always the prude. And you wondered why I had

to fuck around on you." He turns, walking over to my shelves where I have pictures of me and Kyle in frames we bought in the past week.

"He looks like a pussy." Brandon runs his finger along the shelf, knocking the frames to the floor one by one.

"He is more man than you will ever be." I run over, bending to pick up the picture from the broken glass.

"I wouldn't do that if I were you." He steps on my hand with his tennis shoe. Twisting, grinding my hand into the glass until I scream out.

"Brandon!"

"That's not how I remember it." He crosses his arms bringing a finger up to his chin. "What can we do? Any ideas?"

"Please stop!" I stay still. The more I move the deeper the glass cuts.

"Nope. Not quite there." He lifts his foot, relieving the pressure from my hand. When I draw it up against my chest, blood instantly trickles down my arm. Before I can wipe it up, Brandon raises his leg and lets it come down, kicking me in the chest, causing me to fly back and my robe to fall open.

"Ohhhhh." I roll to the side and curl up into a ball. "Why?"

"Why?" He stomps over to where I am. "*Why*? Well, let's see. How about maybe starting with...not saying goodbye."

Curled in the ball, I keep myself hidden as I silence my phone. I start to dial 9-1-1, but then remember it's a track phone. Is that service even provided? Looking at my battery I see I only have five percent.

"Or maybe it's the fact that you had me so worried that I looked for you." He's now behind me, standing near my head.

Forgetting 9-1-1, I decide to voice text Kyle. If I call, he may not be able to answer right away, but texts he will see.

Me: Brandon is here. Call 911.

After sending, I hold down the microphone.

"I even called your whore of a sister and wouldn't you know it, she said you got into some design school out west."

He takes another step forward and stands on the hair that is splayed on the floor behind me, having come free from the force of the kick. Slowly, he drags his foot back, pulling, torturing me.

"Brandon, please!"

I bring my other hand up to swat him away, but he keeps pulling until I'm stretched out, having no choice but to push myself in the direction he's pulling me.

"Does that hurt?" His laugh is now psychotic. "You know what hurts? Me losing my job because I flew out west. I looked up that old lady's daughter and found out that you never contacted her. You never went to school."

He bends down, wrapping a hand around my hair. "But just so you know, this hurts too." He picks my head up and slams it back down.

I close my eyes.

"Don't you fucking pass out on me you little bitch!" He releases my hair, letting my head fall to the floor.

"Please. I can't..." I roll over to protect my phone.

"Yep. I lost my job, which means I couldn't afford to pay *our* house payments. Remember that house? The one you had to have? The one in that fucking neighborhood you wanted *our* kids to grow up in?" He bends down, grabs me by the arm and jerks me to my feet.

Love Conquer

"So, tell me, Nina. What's so fucking special about *this* house?" He pushes me through the broken glass, but this time I don't call out. I know better.

"It's not mine."

He holds one arm behind my back and pushes me to the kitchen.

"Grab me one of those beers in there."

"I can't..." I reply, realizing my mistake as soon as the words leave my mouth.

"Use your ha—" He yanks me around, causing the phone to fly under the table. "God dammit! You stupid bitch."

Not thinking and not caring about what will happen next, I dive for the phone and hit the arrow, sending the voice message.

Kyle.

Taking the phone from my hands, he sees who I messaged and throws his head back, laughing. "You really think he is going to save you, don't you? Your knight in shining armor?"

"He's more than you ever thought you could be. You will *never* be him."

He takes the hand that has my phone and slams it against my cheek. "He's not coming, stupid cunt! I'm all you got."

Blood fills my mouth, the metallic taste too much to handle. I know I shouldn't do it, but right now, I don't care. I'm going to fight and I'll do whatever it takes to make it through this. I'm a survivor.

"If you touch him I swear to God I will find a way to end you. I will make your life miserable." I spit blood in his face.

"I'm going to let that one slide." He turns his cheek. "Lick it off."

"No!"

"Now."

"I said no!"

"This guy? Kyle, is it?" He flips through his phone. "Yep, it says right here. Kyle Lewis. Thirty years old." He looks up. "Little too old for you, don't you think?" He shrugs. "To each his own. Anyways, let's see, owns Woody's. Works as the lead foreman at WilliamSon Construction." He clicks his phone and slides it in his back pocket. "Or maybe it should now read former lead foreman at WilliamSon Construction." He gets nose to nose with me. "He's not coming for you babe. He's dead."

"Wh-what?" I'm in shock.

He's messing with you. Kyle isn't dead.

"The ambulance should be arriving right about..." He looks at his watch. "...now." His grin is pure evil. "It was pretty easy, really. Security sucks around your town, and people just leave shit out in the open for any crazy person to mess with equipment or, let's say, a faulty beam. Heavy enough to cause permanent damage or even kill someone."

Kyle isn't dead!

"You bastard!" I shove him backwards. "You are a sick liar!"

"Are you sure about that?" He pulls a scanner out of his back pocket and turns it on. "Let's listen." He flips through the frequencies until he finds the one he wants. "For your listening pleasure."

I can't believe what I'm hearing.

Accident.

WilliamSon Construction.

En route to hospital.

Critical.

Love Conquer

"You bastard!" I haul back and slap his face. "Why? Why would you do that?" I slap him again. He catches my hand.

"Wrong move, babe."

He grabs me by the shoulders, flinging me across the room.

"Why would I do that?" He stomps over to where I'm lying. My will to fight back is fading. "You're mine. Do you understand me? Mine." He stomps on my leg with the heel of his shoe.

"Fuck!" I cry out.

"Babe, I haven't even begun to start with you." He lowers himself to the floor, a knee on either side of me.

"Brandon, please." I beg.

It's my last fight. It's all I have to give.

One hand.

Then the other.

The pressure is too much to bear.

He's fading.

I'm fading.

Numb.

Darkness.

KYLE

"Kyle! Wake up, man." I hear a voice and feel hands. "Come on. Wake up." Lee's voice is clearer now.

Blinking a few times, I open my eyes and see part of the crew standing over me. "You guys standing around on the job again?" I try to joke but know something is off. My head is killing me.

"We called 9-1-1. They are on their way." Lee tries to fill in the blanks.

911?

The beam.

A crash.

Drew!

"Where's Drew?" I sit up a little too fast. "Fuck!" My hands instantly fly to my head.

"We think you just got grazed, but hit your head pretty hard coming down, which caused you to black out." Lee continues to give me the facts. All but the one I want.

"Okay, whatever." I wave him off. "How's Drew? He was on the way out. Right by the beam."

"Drew's down, man." Lee looks across the room. "I'm not going to lie. It's pretty bad."

Trying to stand up, I lean on Lee for balance. The sound of sirens gets closer.

"He's right over here!" I hear someone yell.

My eyes follow the voice and I see Drew lying lifeless. "Drew!" I shout. Pushing Lee away I take off across the room, ignoring the pounding in my brain, forcing my feet to move faster.

"Sir excuse me. We need to get through." The paramedics come barreling in with a gurney.

I step to the left, letting them pass as I stand helpless, watching my friend get checked out.

"He's stable," one calls out as the others go to get him on the gurney. "Call it in! Let's go. Lift on three."

Love Conquer

"Let's move." Another directs, and I watch as Drew is taken out on a stretcher, not moving.

"Is he going to be okay?" I holler after them as they load him up.

"Probably just a severe concussion, but we don't know the severity of the fall. He had his hardhat on, so that's a plus." He hops in and I'm about to climb in behind him.

"I'm sorry, but you'll have to follow behind." He starts to shut the door.

"His wife is in labor!" I shout.

"Excuse me?" He swings it back open.

"Aubrey Williams. She's at the hospital now. She's in labor. He was trying to get to her," I say hurriedly.

"We will get him there." He pulls the door shut.

"Lee! I'm heading to the hospital. You know what to do man. Do it." I jump in the truck and pull out my phone to call Niki.

I see a text from Nina.

Brandon is here. Call 911.

"Son of a bitch!" I throw it in gear and head her way. Dialing 911 as I go, shouting Nina's address to dispatch, unable to say much more than to send help. I quickly send Niki a voice message to get to Nina's ASAP.

I can't think straight. My head is pounding. I need to get to my girl. My grip tightens. My stomach clenches.

Hold on, baby.

Drawing in a ragged breath I push play to listen to the voice message. I can't believe what I'm hearing. Her screams. Her pleas as they fall upon deaf ears. I wasn't there when she needed me.

I throw the phone on the dash and grip the wheel with both hands. My jaw pops as I clench my teeth.

I make it to her house in record time and I'm the first one there. No vehicles, and darkness envelopes the house. I'm not sure what I'm running in to, but I don't think. I sprint across the lawn and slam open the door.

Brandon is on top of Nina, beating the life right out of her.

"Motherfucker!" I roar, grabbing him by the neck and throwing him off.

"Little too late." He nods towards her, laughing at me.

Her beaten body lies still.

Lifeless.

"Nooooooooo!" I scream and run to her. I try to find a pulse but I'm afraid to touch her. "Baby, please. Nina! Answer me!" I cry out as I squeeze her bloody hand in mine.

He's a dead man. One minute I'm holding Nina's hand and the next thing I know, I'm on top of him. I land the first punch, which knocks him out, but that's not enough.

Life for a life.

One punch. Blood.

Two.

Three. Teeth break.

Four.

Five. Bones shatter.

Blood is everywhere. My hands are numb, like my mind. My head is swimming, I'm starting to see double.

"Jonestown PD. Hands up!"

I don't stop. I can't stop. He has to pay.

"Hands up, now!"

"She's alive." I hear someone else call out.

"What?" I turn around and all guns are pointed on me. Raising my hands. "She's alive?"

"No thanks to you." An officer comes up to me, locking my hands behind my back. He pushes me to the floor and begins to pat me down.

She's alive.

She's alive.

She's alive.

I struggle, I have to get to her.

"Wait! Wait!" I begin to fight back. "I didn't hurt her. You've got it all wrong. I need to go to the hospital. Please just let me go!"

"Sir, you need to calm down. We have to assess the scene." Another officer comes up. helping me stand.

"We need to get a statement first."

"I can't. Fuck that! I have to go with her." I watch as they load her up and begin to wheel her out.

"No! Please! She's my life," I beg, the cuffs cutting into my wrists as I try to move my arms. "I can't let anything happen to her!" I yell as they walk me outside. I see them bring another gurney toward the house. That asshole. "Please!"

Nothing.

The ambulance doors close with my whole world in the back.

"I need to go with her! Why won't anyone listen to me?" My voice is raw from yelling.

"I'm sorry. You can't go anywhere till we get a statement." The officer says as he puts me in the back of a cruiser.

My head hangs in defeat.

Then go.
Save her.
Help her.
Fight, Nina. Fight!zzzzzzzzzz

Chapter 29

KYLE

After I pleaded for the police to listen to the voice message, they let me give a quick statement and head to the hospital.

I drive up to the emergency room door and jump out, throwing the keys to the security guard. "Tow it. Keep it. I don't care."

"Sir! You can't park here!" he hollers after me.

Running through the doors, I head to the help desk.

"Where's Nina?" They don't answer. "Dammit!" I slam my fist on the counter. "Nina Sanders was brought in here over an hour ago. Where is she?"

"You are?" a woman asks as she spins around in her chair.

"Her boyfriend." I pant trying to catch my breath.

"I'm sorry. We can't give you that information." She turns back around and continues to talk to one of the nurses, like nothing is wrong. Like my whole world isn't crumbling around me.

"Listen." I interrupt, raising my voice again. "I have to find her!"

She just stares at me. No emotions. Her eyes never blink.

Please! To anyone who is listening. Please, let me find her.

"This woman I'm going to spend the rest of my life with was beaten, nearly to death and I had to watch as her lifeless body lay there in front of me as they took her away. So, don't tell me to calm down!" I rasp out. "I know she's here, so either you start talking or I'll go in every last room until I find her."

A sympathetic look, crosses her face.

"So please." I hold my hands together, pleading. "Tell me where I can find her."

"Well..." She types something on her keyboard. "I can't tell you which room she is in, but what I *can* tell you is she is in intensive care."

I slap the counter and point at her. "You are the best!" I run through the waiting room, bypassing the elevators and taking the stairs two at a time.

Nina! I'm coming, baby!

Throwing the doors open, I run down the hall and to the nurse's station. "Nina Sanders. I know she is up here. *Please*, which room?"

"Sir, calm down." An older nurse comes over. "We have patients who are trying to recover. Patients who need round the clock care in their fight to live. So, please do us a favor and calm down."

"I'm sorry. I need to see Nina Sanders." I hand my head, knowing my girl is one of those fighting for her life.

"Okay, good. Now who are you to the patient?" Her kind voice asks me.

"Kyle Lewis." I lift my head, hopeful. *Please. Please. I hold my breath.*

"Oh! Her sister said you would be here. Room 512. She's

sleeping."

"Thank you. Thank you so much." I back away, releasing a relieved sigh, and take off, trying not to run. My heart pounds harder, the closer I get.

506. Thump.

508. Thump.

510. Thump.

512. Thump. Thump.

Her door is open and I can see her from the hall. The glow of the machines cast an eerie light on her face.

Wires.

Monitors.

Beeping.

"Kyle?" Niki gets up from a chair next to the bed to come talk to me, with Gavin close behind as she rushes to me. "She has a severe concussion and loss of oxygen to the brain." She's distraught and tears fill her eyes. "She's going to make it, but she hasn't woken up yet and they don't know why." She turns to Gavin, falling into his arms.

"I'm sorry Niki, I'm so sorry." I try to say, but my voice shakes as I look into the face of the sister of the girl I love, but didn't protect. "I didn't get there sooner. I tried. I— "

"Shhh. Kyle, don't." She leans in to hug me, before releasing and looking up at me. "It's not your fault! You made it, you got help! Don't you see, if it wasn't for you…it could have been so much worse. So, don't."

"Okay. Can I?" I nod to the chair.

"Sure. We are going to go check in on Drew and Aubrey."

"Shit. I almost forgot."

"Drew has a concussion and severe laceration on his right

arm." She turns to Gavin and smiles. "Hardhat saved his life." She looks back to me and nods. "Once he woke up and he was checked out, they agreed to set up a room for him and Aubrey."

Safety first.

"Did she have the baby?"

"Not yet, but soon." She walks back up to Nina's bed and weaves her hand in between the wires to hold her sister's hand. "Nina, Kyle's here, sweetie. I'm going to check on Aubrey." She bends to give her battered face a tender kiss.

"Tell Drew..." I begin to tear up. Drew has been there through it all. Losing him would have been like losing a brother.

"I know. I get it." Niki heads for the door, Gavin right behind, wrapping an arm around her waist to guide her in the right direction. They shut the door as they leave.

Scooting the chair forward, I lean over the bed and lay my hand out, palm up. Unsure if she can hear me. Unsure of what to say. So, I start with the truth.

Hand hug.

"Baby, I was so worried. I thought..." I begin to sob at the thought of losing her, the one person who makes me feel like I matter. "I thought I lost you."

I take a minute to compose myself. "He won't hurt you ever again. I made sure of that," I confess. "I hurt him baby. I hurt him like he hurt you. I made him pay. I didn't kill him, but Nina, I wanted to. I wanted him to die for what he did to you. For putting his hands on you. Not just tonight, but for every single time he hurt you. With his hands. With his words. For making you doubt how incredible you are, how talented and gorgeous and brave and smart. But it's over now. You'll never doubt those things again."

Love Conquer

I reach my hand up to brush the hair out of her eyes. "Baby, I know I'm supposed to let you sleep, but I'm a selfish bastard. I need to know if you are really okay. I need to know you're here with me. If you please wake up, I promise, I'll remind you of those things every day."

Reaching down, I take her bandaged hand and place it in mine. I lower my head to the bed. I close my eyes and do something I haven't done since my dad died. I pray. "Nina, don't leave me. Don't ever leave me." I feather light kisses up her arm. "I can't live without you. I wouldn't even know where to begin a life without you. My heart, it's wide open now and *you* are the reason why."

Squeeze.

NINA

Lights. Monitors. Blood.

Lights. They're so bright. Too bright to open my eyes. I just need to sleep, to fall into the night.

Monitors. I can hear them, the sound of my life beeping throughout the room. The reminder that this wasn't for nothing. This was for me. For him, my future.

Blood. I can feel it on my skin, taste it in my mouth. I feel so dirty; I want to wash away the past and move on to my future.

I've never felt more alone than I do right now. Trapped in the darkness that took me over. Brandon did this to me. He tried to take what was left and I wouldn't give it to him.

I fought.
Even though I couldn't see him. I felt him there. Saving me from the hands of the demon that tried to bring me down.

I reached for him. When I thought I was going to die, I reached for his hand. I knew if I had it, everything would be okay.

His kisses.
His touch.
His hand.
Hand hug.
My hand.
His hand.
Squeeze.

"Nina?" Kyle whispers as he gives me a squeeze back, causing me to wince. "Come back to me baby. Show me you are okay."

I'm trying, Kyle.
Squeeze.

"I feel you. I know you're there. Just open those beautiful emerald eyes of yours. Please, Nina, for me."

"Kyle." I speak his name before I can see him. Opening my eyes, I wince, it hurts too much.

"Oh shit!" I hear him get up and run around the bed to flip a switch. "They're out now. It's safe."

That's my Kyle. Always knowing just what I need.

Blinking.
Squeeze.

"That's right, Nina. Open them." I hear him beg.

"Chivalry isn't dead," I croak out as my eyes flutter open.

"What was that?" He leans to put his ear by my mouth.

"Chivalry isn't dead. The lights." I try to pick up my hand

to point but it's too much, my arm feels like it has lead weights attached to it.

"Nope." He begins to laugh. "It's not."

"Baby, what happened tonight." His body begins to shake. "I wasn't there to prevent it, but I tried. I tried so hard to stop it."

"You got my text." I barely get the words out, my throat raw and my mouth like cotton.

"Yes. I did. You fought baby. You fought him off and we won." He shakes his head. "If you wouldn't have...if there was no text...Nina, you were very lucky."

"Bran—"

"He's in here somewhere, but don't worry. The sheriff's office has deputies watching over him." He reassures me. "That asshole is getting nowhere near you, ever again."

"What's going to happen?" I ask the question I'm not sure I want the answer to.

"Well, *if* he ever wakes up, he will be prosecuted for attempted murder."

"What do you mean? Wakes up?" I struggle to remember what happened. I fought back, but he was on top of me, I used everything I had left to fight. But then it all went dark.

"I beat him bad. I used every ounce of anger I had and pounded him until they pulled me off. I was going to kill him. I didn't care." He turns his face, unable to look at me. Not from the bruises, but from his guilt. Fear that I'll be afraid of him. I see it in his eyes. "I've got blood on my hands and I would have let it settle in my soul if that is what it would have taken to keep you safe."

I slowly bring my hand to his face, ignoring the pain, just

to let this man know how much he isn't like him. "Don't! You are not him. You are a so much more." I lay a kiss on his hand despite the pressure from puckering up being so painful. "These hands healed me, not hurt me.

"I thought I wanted to disappear, escape who I had become, but all I wanted, what I needed, was to be found...by you." I squeeze Kyle's hand. "Don't you get that? You saved me from the shell of the person I had become and filled me with the hope I thought was lost. Piecing me back together with who you are and who you know I can be. A love like this is real...I know that now...because of *you*."

"I love you, Nina," he says, laying his hand in my lap, palm open.

Hand hug.

"I love you too." I take his hand in mine.

Squeeze.

6 MONTHS LATER

NINA

When do the words "I love you" mean everything? When they are said by someone who means them. Someone whose words and touch have healed me. Taught me what love truly feels like.

Trust.

No more blurring of the lines. No wrongs. Only rights. And who I've become is who I was always meant to be. A sister. A friend. A girlfriend. Smart. Brave. Creative. Someone I left buried deep inside, because I was forced to. But not anymore. I'm all that and more, because of the love and support of those around me. Because I refuse to be less ever again.

Pride.

I escaped and nearly lost, but I fought and I won. My reward...

Love.

I feel the bright lights on my face and I look down at the man in front of me, on one knee, waiting for my answer.

"Yes." I nod.

He smiles up at me.

"Yes! A million times yes!" I cry.

Jumping to his feet, in a move I'm sure I'll see later on the dance floor, Kyle picks me up and swings me around. My arms around his neck. His around my waist.

"You can't get rid of me now." He slowly comes to a stop and lowers me to the dance floor. "This ring." He reaches up and pulls my hand down, twirling my ring between his fingers. He locks our hands. "It says we are forever."

Happiness.

"Forever is a long time." I pull my other hand down and find the one place it was made to be. Two hands woven to become one.

"With you, it will never be enough." He wraps both our arms around his back as we slowly begin to move.

Always.

"Hey you two. Sorry to crash your party, but you have a couple of surprise guests." Niki sneaks over, breaking up our little private reception.

"Who do you think it could be?" I tease Kyle, knowing exactly who it is. Excited, I pull him behind me and up to the VIP section where all our friends and family wait.

"No telling." He follows me up, once again being the perfect gentleman.

"Well, here they are..."

"Jack? Tristan?" He looks down at me. "You did this, didn't you?"

I nod excitedly. "You mom said they were in town and since you invited your parents here for my end of semester celebration, I thought why not them."

Love Conquer

"Kyle." Jack walks up first, with Tristan behind him.

"Hey brother." Kyle gives them both a hug.

Times may have been rough, but after a few get-togethers everything really started falling into place and surprisingly enough, Tristan has become a great friend.

Forgiveness.

"Well, come on over." Kyle waves them to our VIP booths Gavin so graciously got the owner to donate for the special occasion. I just didn't know how *special* it really was going to be.

"I think this calls for a round of drinks!" Kyle searches the floor. "Hey where's Lee?"

"He disappeared downstairs right before you stole the show out there," Jen replies.

"Figures he would find a way to get out of buying a round," Kyle laughs.

"I'll get this one!" Gavin pipes up. "Margaritas for everyone!" He shouts and the table erupts in approval.

I look around, the tables filled with smiling faces and laughter. The man beside me, my everything. His parents and family. Drew and Aubrey. My sister and best friend across from us with her husband. *Husband!* I still can't believe she really did it. I'm still not sure why anyone would sign on for a lifetime of mornings with her, before she's caffeinated. But I love her, I love him and I love that they showed me what true love looks like. I knew they would end up tying the knot, I just didn't expect it to be at an impromptu end of summer barbeque.

We may not have parents anymore, but we've found ourselves an incredible family right here in this collection of people. People willing to support and fight for one another and for what's right. The broken, the brokenhearted, the abused, the healed, friends turned

Family.

"Hey you." Kyle leans over and whispers in my ear, interrupting my thoughts. "You ready to go?"

"Why, fiancé, is that your way of trying to get me alone?" I tease and place my lips to his.

"It is now." He jokes, before deepening the kiss, causing everyone to whistle and cheer."

"On that note, we're gonna call it a night." Kyle announces as he stands from the booth and holds his hand out to me. "Thanks everyone for coming and to Gavin for hooking us up! Feel free to stay as long as you like."

It's my turn to say something and I hope I can talk without crying. "Thank you, everyone for being here to support us. For everything." I manage to get out.

We get all the hugs and congratulations out of the way, his mom making me promise to take care of her boy, Niki trying to give me "marital bed tips" I think she called them.

"Finally." Kyle says as he shuts his door, after making sure to escort me in the truck first. "I'm ready to be alone with you."

He places his hand on the console, palm up and I put my left hand in his.

Squeeze.

He plays with my ring with his thumb. "I like this new addition to our hand hug."

"Me too." I smile, my heart full.

We pull into the drive before I realize where we are, the tire swing illuminated in the headlights.

The cabin.

Love Conquer

We've been splitting our time up between our places, not wanting to rush anything.

Walking me up to the porch, he takes a seat on one of the two rockers, pulling me to him. The light catches something shiny as he places it in my hand.

Holding my palm in front of me, I see it's a key.

"You already have my ring." He explains. "That's a promise from a husband to a wife. You've had my heart for a while now. That's from a man to a woman. But this...this key. Its every dream I ever had, it's the future I envisioned. It's my father's legacy. And now it'll be mine *and* yours. It'll be ours."

Speechless and overwhelmed for what I feel for this incredible man, I blink back tears.

"But I want this to be our home. I want to sit on the porch and drink Lipton tea with you, I wanna watch our babies play in this yard." He tells me.

"Kyle." I whisper.

"I know you just got your independence back and I'm not trying to take that away. You know I would never do that. We can keep your place too, if you want. And I know we aren't married yet. But this isn't just my cabin anymore, it's ours." He rambles.

"Kyle." I interrupt. "Wherever you are, is where I want to be. I love you. And I would be honored to share your dream."

"I love you too, Nina." He lifts me into his arms before carrying me over the threshold. "Welcome home baby."

Home.

The End

Acknowledgements

First off, I want to thank my Mom. Without her. I wouldn't be writing, like for real...she got me a Mac, yo!

Brittany, I dedicated this book to you, but the late nights reading chapter after chapter. Listening to me whine and cry... it takes a special friend to deal with my craziness. Thank you! #BFF #TwinningIsWinning #CalmTheFuckDown

Stephanie, you whore! My friend, my critique partner... What would I do without you? Probably binge watch Netflix. #100 #Whore #HippyShit #WorldDomination

Christy, I dig you, ho! (insert evil laugh here). Writing retreat at the Pastore's! . #GirlsRunTheWorld #WeComing

Kelly, Without you, I would probably be late getting up. Thanks for being my alarm! #MorningsSuck #coffeesaveslives

To my VIP Review Team...Thanks for loving my words! For being patient! And for me always being late with ARC's! xoxo

To all my wonderful Sweethart's... you guys sure know how to whore me out! I heart you guys! You ladies, I love you so much. Every time I get a tag... I smile. #sharingiscaring

Dani, I don't know how you do it, but thank you for dealing with my crazy. Thank you for having my back and not letting me give up. PS I still think I'm cursed. I <3 you so hard! #MadLove

And to some very special people in my book world: Jen, Happy Birthday! Thanks for being my barista! #coffeetime

It's an important job and somebody had to do it. Niki, you are the shit! #kissyface Stracey, Thank you for loving my words. #bookfrinds4life Tammy, without you my world would be a mess. #eagleeye.

After Hours Book House– I love you all. Thank you for all the love and support. #AHBH

Let's not forget Spotify... Thanks for having a song for every one of my moods.

To my husband and kids... Thanks to you guys... I DID IT! Mommy's back!

To all the bloggers... As a reader, I enjoy you. As a writer, I adore you. Everything you do is for the love of books... thanks!

About the Author

Cary Hart hails from the Midwest. A sassy, coffee drinking, sometimes sailor swearing, Spotify addict, lover of all things books!

When not pushing women down the stairs in the fictional world, Cary has her hands full. Soccer mom in all sense of the word to two wild and crazy, spoiled kiddos, and wife to the most supportive husband. In addition to writing full time, she enjoys binge watching Netflix, laying around in her hammock and baking up cookies for her family and friends.

Cary writes real, raw romance! In her stories the characters deal with life's everyday struggles and unwanted drama, they talk about the ugly and they become the broken. Everyone deserves a happy ending, but sometimes before you can appreciate the light, there has to be darkness.

Growing up, if someone would have told her she would become a writer, she wouldn't have believed them. It wasn't until she got her hands on her first romance novel, that the passion grew. Now she couldn't imagine her life any other way - she's living her dream.

Cary's Newsletter
The Pulse: *http://eepurl.com/cffmYX*

Or follow her on her website
www.authorcaryhart.com

Made in the USA
Lexington, KY
18 December 2018